T

Who don't know whe

the same direction as the wind.
The people who are ever-flowing.
People like Roxanne.

First paperback edition October 2019

Book design by Faran Riley

ISBN 9781694353917 (paperback)

www.brownjade.com

Author's Notes

Vienna is a fiction experiment that I decided to undertake as a way to challenge my previous unpublished compositions. The story itself follows no structure or controlled premise, it is simply for a personalized experience between the reader and the page.

The book is written in three parts, each chapter introduces a new narrator, with 4 consistent narrators in each section - Cinth, Delilah, Gerry & Tob (joined), and Nolan. There are no rules when addressing this piece of literature, meaning, it doesn't have to be read in chronological order. Each chapter is its own story, and I encourage others to challenge themselves in rouletting the various narrations, or passing a chapter along to a friend without previous context. Since each story migrates into one another, I also urge readers to become well acquainted with the diverse voices.

Vienna explores themes of self-destruction, mental heath, and substance abuse, but wasn't built upon those ideas.

Fiction it is, but fiction it is also not.

Vienna

By Jade Brown

1
The Most Likely

Cinth

Me: Hey

A white van decorated in graffiti caressed the edge of the sidewalk. It was large enough to hold my body weight, and eccentric enough to fool any cop that questioned whether or not I owned the vehicle. Only ten minutes went by, and I was already playing text-tag with no one. Was she ignoring me? I didn't want to look into her apartment, but my eyes made up their mind before my thoughts could. The curtains were drawn, but I could see the miniature floor lamp that stood in her living room, exuding its vibrant pink light.

Me: I'm here.

It wasn't purely physical with Vienna. When I first saw her, I had this undeniable urge to hover. Clearly. I was standing outside of her apartment in the Lower East Side at 1am. Vienna disregards her flaws but has so many, and I think that's the reason I find myself competing with other people. There is something so sexy about a person who is filled to the brim with errors but acts as though they carry nothing but self-glee. I lick my lips at the notion of being part of her selfish fulfillment. I secretly wanted to be on that list, but I know that Vienna has no time for that. She has no time for people like me.

An hour went by and I considered going home. I wondered what would happen if I chucked my phone at the homeless dude laid up against the building. Vienna hates when I get mad. She would always bring up how the skin around my nose turns magenta, and that is very much a *white people* thing. Even though Vienna's complexion is champagne mocha, I can always tell when she's upset. She has these eyes that tell me stories that I don't want to hear, but I'm forced to read every time I look at her. It's seldom, but there are moments when her eyes spell out nothing but sorrow, even during times where she utters nothing but happiness. I told her she doesn't have to cover up pain that way, that I always see it, but she continues to deny it.

I shouldn't be here. I should've called to see if she would be home or called to see if she'd want to see me. I haven't heard from her in a few days. The last time I saw her, I could've sworn she had tears in her eyes, and she hopped on top of me trying to see where my morality lies. She wasn't drunk, but she should've been. It would've been easier to calm her down, to let her know that that wasn't the move she'd want to make, and mistakes pile up higher than a New York City apartment ceiling. That was the first time I tried to tell her I loved her. Every moment since then, I've awaited the chance to see her face to face again, so I could let her know how I really feel. That chance never came.

I spoke to my dad about Vienna, and he told me that once a woman is scorned, she is unobtainable. When that sentence left his lips, I demanded that he put my mother on the phone. My mother told me that Vienna is filled with too many questions that need no answers, and I should've given her up a long time ago. At that point, I hung up. I'm not sure why I search for approval in people besides myself, why does anyone? I figured I shouldn't yearn for validation in areas in my life, especially when it comes to love because it will always remain irrational. No one will understand my feelings for Vienna because no one looks at Vienna through me. No one thinks of Vienna the way my brain engulfs her, and no one has ever made her tender like I have, even if I convince myself of that.

"Cinth?" my mind was cynical, allowing me to believe that Vienna's voice was calling my name. I shoved my body from off of the van, and forced my vision to settle down. I glanced over, trying to see if the homeless man was still hurdled up against the building, but instead, I found myself becoming unraveled.

"Vienna."

"What are you doing here?" she wore an olive green baseball cap that created a shadow above her large eyes, which made it even more difficult for me to analyze her.

"I came to see you," this answer could either flatter her or make her feel highly uncomfortable.

"Come upstairs with me, it's cold," she took me by my hand, pulling me in her direction. I wasn't sure why, but I felt as though I built my sanctuary near this van. I could spend hours just looking up in hopes and uncertainty as to whether or not I'd see her again.

Before we entered her apartment, I could already smell her cedar scented candle burning into the narrow hallway. My senses took me back to the times I'd scowl at her to blow out her candles before leaving her apartment. She walked ahead of me, flinging her jacket onto her faux suede couch, exposing her navy colored tank top and fitted jeans. She ripped her cap off and ran her bare fingertips through her brown curls. I knew by the way she noticeably shifted her weight from side to side that she was inviting me to unfold her. This was a very *Vienna thing*. I turned in the opposite direction toward her coat hanger, and started to unzip my hoodie. The goosebumps on my arms were bulging out, and it wasn't a reaction to the freezing apartment.

Vienna was beautiful but not in the way that gasps for attention, or the way that gets cat-called regularly, she was subtle. I would notice the way people's eyes would sway on the train platform whenever she passed by. She carried herself with so much respect that folks wouldn't dare to make a comment. It's a complete ego booster to know that I could get along with someone who silently infatuated others, and I wanted to mutter in their ears that she's just as exciting as she looks. Her body doesn't fill out all the clothes she puts on, but God, does know how to wear them. I'm sure she's convinced that I'm only keen on taking them off, but I love to look at her while she's concentrated on nothing but our hands intertwined.

"What do you want to listen to?" she reached into her back pocket, pulling out her cell phone, her fingers flicking and typing. Texting. I couldn't help but question who she was talking to and if they were better than me.

"I'll listen to whatever you want," even though I'd love to just replay her breathing through the stereo.

"How about we listen to traffic?" Vienna tossed her phone onto her sofa and began making her way toward me.

"Vien-" she threw her arms around my neck, tugging me into her chest. Our breast touched as her plump lips drew into mine. She knows how to kiss me in ways that make me forget why I ever came, and why I began stalking her.

In my mind, she was undressing me, and we were on our way to her bedroom, but this time was different. She wanted me to make all the first moves. My feet sunk into the ground, and she continued to push up against me, forcing my closeted aggression to arise. She jumped up, swinging her legs around my waist, steering my arms to cup her cheeks. I carried her to the sofa, steadily placing her on her back as her breath filled the room. My hand ran into her hair, scrunching her head back as her mouth parted open just enough for me to drip my tongue into hers. I slid my free hand down her thigh and pushed her legs further apart, pressing my pelvis up to hers while lightly tapping.

"This is what you want?" I asked her.

"Yes!" she groaned.

"I can't," I pushed myself up, leaning over her perplexed glare.

"Why?"

"Because I love you, Vienna," I actually said it.

Her eyes told me nothing. They didn't tell me that she felt

the same way, they didn't even tell me she hated me.

2
The Lip Muncher
Bobby

Sometimes she comes in looking for a beer and other times, she tries to dissolve in thin air. I told her it ain't possible. There are days where her money sticks out of her pocket so bad that it exposes the white cotton fabric that no one should see. She'll drop a dollar or ten here and there, and the men in the shop will go wild. They'll fight one another to stab the area the buck fell cause they all wanted to see her arched back rotate downward.

She's not a quarter found in a piggy bank, but she's not a penny either. She don't know how beautiful she is, and I would anticipate her arrival at times, her need for a quick buzz. Whenever she approaches the counter, she bats those crow-feather eyelashes, and I'm about to lose my job. She handed me her bank card once to ring up a case of Blue Moons, and I read her name out loud back to her. She giggled at me butchering it, and I already knew that I wasn't one of those cultured types she typically waltzes in with.

"Vi-Enna. Like Emma but with an N," she lengthened her arms out along the counter.

"I never met anyone with that name," her lanky arms were extended out so bad that I questioned if she wanted me to pull her in.

"I can tell."

Most of the time, I'll see her coming in with the she-he. I thought it was a man at first cause it was real tall with a shaved cut and tattoos up n' down its arms. Good looking. It wasn't until the one time they came in, and I could see its hard tits damn-near kissing the cotton. I wasn't freaked out because I'm not a homophobe, and I can appreciate people's sexual orientation, but I have never been around anything like that. Everyone assumes when a person lives in New York they're open to everything, but where I'm from, I'd never see a bulldike with someone like Vienna.

I'm not inexperienced when it comes to dating, but I know I can't muster up enough courage to ask her out. I knew that once I was in front of her curvaceous lips, it'd be impossible to focus on constructing a sentence. I'll be loosening that knotted top of hers in my mind, and she'll be sitting back allowing me to. She's always showing that belly button that likes to peer above her pants clasp. I don't know if she's confessing to me or trying to break a twenty. I want her to want me because everybody wants her. Maybe I have something to prove that could make the difference.

3
The Unintentional Cutout
Delilah

One day, Nolan shouted Vienna's name in bed, and that was when my blueprint to kill her sprung. She drags her feet around, and I'm sure it's her way of forcing the floor to screech for her. Vienna has to remind herself how much the world engulfs her salaciousness because her presence doesn't make up for missed connections. I never tried to be Vienna's friend because she marinates in sin and bastes in unforgivingness. I told her that I pray for her from time to time, and she rebuked my condolences. What do I condole? Her existence. I know that beneath those almond plastered eyes, there's something that lacks. Other people may not see that, but I do.

I'm not in love with Nolan, but I give him my companionship. He knows that he is a toxin in my heavily molded lifestyle. My family will never accept the dark boy who dropped out of High School to pursue a far-fetched career in music. I muttered to Nolan that punk is dead, and that he could only succeed in bad acoustic covers of songs that were never that great. Nolan is also a stubborn person. I tell him that he should abandon all the feelings he has for Vienna, but he continues to exchange both of our bodily fluids through him. I can't go on strike and revolt against his parts because if there is anything the Lord knows, it's my uncontrollable need for venom.

Vienna isn't that good looking. Her curls are short and they latch onto an emerald dye that never wanted to touch her in the first place. Her face is simply lips that don't move enough because if they did, maybe people would see just how much feces reside on her teeth. Her body is adjacent to the definition of *Okay*, and sullen is her forever mood. Her clothes are always too tight or too loose, and she doesn't seem to care who is looking, as long as they're looking at her. Her greatest downfall is attention, and I try to give her tips on how to be less apparent but apparently, I'm unqualified.

"What?" I don't know why I can't stop hiking me and Vienna up on a cork-board, forcing her to decompose like the soot she is. Nolan always internalizes my hatred and throws it back at me during our most intimate times.

"Nothing," I perched up onto my pillow, his head still cupped my in-between.

"C'mon Dell, don't be this way. I see it all over your face." his fingertips drew on my inner thigh.

"Why are you looking at me?"

"I like seeing the faces you make," he kissed the invisible drawing.

First Corinthians 6:18, *Flee from sexual immorality. All other sin a person commits are outside the body, but whoever sins sexually, sins against their own body.* Vienna allows people to enter her like a congregation lining up to inhale the blood of our savior. Where is the self-respect in that? A woman who values herself is a woman worth valuing, my daddy always preaches this. Vienna has allowed people of all kind to guzzle her aromas, and her beaus build up and peel off onto the people that want nothing to do with her. Like me. I tell Nolan every time he walks into my home that he needs to wash off her paw prints and brush her rupturing riddles off his tongue. No matter how long he soaks in my holy water, I still smell her.

Nolan's disorder eases my compulsion, that's why I need him. Every extremity he experiences transitions with his want for me. There are days where he can tell me exactly how he feels because he is propped up on exultation. He'll make love to me, call me by the abbreviation that he created, and swallow my yearnings to rearrange his crooked alignments. My therapist chants that I control everything in my life, and that alone should nurture my OCD, but what my therapist doesn't know is that the thing I believe sedates me the most is the thing that I have no handle on. No matter how many times I warn Nolan, he keeps exhausting himself with the idea of Vienna, and I'm left fixing muddled lines of communication.

My prerequisite for Nolan was to remain filtered. Even though I can re-purify myself after our amorous acts, I needed him to comply. My tics resurrect whenever I see Vienna outlined in his pupils. She has coerced Nolan into her swarm of polygamous dogs, and he's fetching far beyond his leashes leeway. My faith has surged from my fingertips into Nolan's back, and yet he still rebels against me. Nolan tells me that physically, I am his type, I've got the beauty and grace that Vienna could never match. My daddy said that my eyes are the color of the water that Jesus walked on, and any person who stares long enough could be saved. I never asked my daddy what will happen if someone can't manage to make eye contact.

"Does it feel good?" Nolan rose up, leaning his chin

against my pelvis.

"Yeah," I grinned down. Nolan traced my bent leg and took hold of my foot. "Nolan!"

"Sorry," I yanked my toes away and pushed myself onto my calves. This way, my feet were nowhere in his sight. "I forgot."

"No feet stuff."

"Dell, should I go?"

This has been going on just under a year. Nolan knew the next man I would give myself to would be the man I would possibly marry. I'm young but prepared for eternal devotion ever since I was born into Christ. Nolan wasn't the primped prince I asked for, but I couldn't get his hickory-toned skin out of my mind. His beard had a hair that never laid, and during our group meetings, my focus would be on it. Every meeting, I'd come in and await that stranded follicle just to stare it down. It wasn't soon after that I realized my fixation on Nolan and his obsessions with Vienna too. Even after the first time we made love, I cut the improper hair from his chin, but I could still see his attention was divided. I don't know why I assumed that hair represented Vienna, maybe I wished it would.

"Don't go, stay put!" I could sense how disheveled my hair was, and my limbs made their own decision to snatch a comb from the bathroom.

"Dell, I think I might head out," I could hear Nolan shouting from my room, but I still needed to complete twelve more strokes.

"Just a minute!" I couldn't rush it, but I couldn't let him go either. I couldn't allow Nolan to leave.

"Dell," I scurried out of the bathroom, almost slipping on my own under garments. I caught myself by the entrance of my room and found Nolan dragging on his jeans.

"Nolan, don't go."

"It's been weird," he reached for his top that hung on the back of my task chair.

She's not even here and she's messing things up. Vienna is interrupting my hair time, my intimacy, and my narcotic. Nolan doesn't have a permanent place to stay, and I couldn't help but to obsess over the possibility of him sleeping with her instead of me. My bed is the only serenity that his body can take, and if he keeps revolving, he'll never become as clean as I need him to be. I deserve to be sanctioned in a column of my own, to be desired, and to be sought after. I live my life dwelling in perfection and all Vienna had to do is tread in mediocrity. People flock to her, but who flocks for me?

"Are you going to spend the night with her?" I questioned. Nolan readjusted his sack beneath his tight denim.

"No, I'm going to Derek's."

"Proverbs 12:22, *The LORD detests lying lips, but he delights in people who are trustworthy.*"

"Dell, I wouldn't lie to you."

"Isaiah 59:15, *Truth is nowhere to be found, and whoever shuns evil becomes a prey.*"

"Stop! Don't do this with me," Nolan picked up his guitar

case and began to head toward the door.

"Nolan, you can't shame me for obsessing over your relationship with her."

"My relationship with Vienna is no different from my relationship with you."

"I know, and that's the issue! I want to at least feel like I'm something more than someone you occasionally sleep with," I began to creep forward as Nolan placed his guitar in front of him like a closed gate.

"It hurts me that you would say that."

I wasn't sure if it was part of Nolan's bipolar disorder, but in tension-filled settings, he retreats to be the sufferer. He continuously uses this tactic with me, and there is no way to go around it. Once Nolan feels as though he has been betrayed in an argument, he buckles. I shouldn't feel his reflecting guilt because I am one of two women, and I should be the one embraced and comforted. Nolan can't be my tranquility because of his imbalance, but I want him to try to disregard his comfort zone like I disregarded my need to brush my hair eight more times.

"It hurts when you look at me because I know you're picturing her."

4
The Revolver
Arion

The last time I saw Vienna, she pecked me goodbye before heading on the J train. Her prodigiously oval sunglasses nearly covered her entire face, and I questioned if I was good enough to walk beside her. I was in a heavy debate as to whether I should stretch my hand out, or if I should continue to mask my emotions under my unbothered facade. She's so beautiful, I would love to hold her hand. I would love to prove to myself that all the self-assertions I utter can take the place of romantic abandonment. When I'm in her presence, she treats me as though I'm worth everything in the world, but when I'm not with her, I am overwhelmed by inferiority.

Me: I was wondering if you wanna get together tonight?

7 hours pass.

Vienna: shit i just saw this.

Me: haha it's cool! You busy?

If I only wanted to sleep with Vienna, then our relationship would be far less complicated. Initially, it was something sexual, but then it slowly progressed into what I assumed was more emotional intimacy. I told her about my need for creative expression, and how I thought moving to New York would somehow miraculously cure my painter's block. Vienna identifies as a doodler, but her doodles are a little more detailed than the average textbook artiste. Art is what brought us together, and I think it's going to be the substructure that I could always come back to. I see art in Vienna, but more so, I see a landscape in us. We just don't always share the same artistic vision.

Me: loading up on ice cream in greenpoint! Think you got a sweet tooth?

2 hours pass.

Me: just left! Maybe we can hang tomorrow.

Vienna warned me that she was a terrible texter, and I believed her. I am only a fraction of her ingenious mind, and I don't want to stifle her intellectual capacity. She also told me that her feelings for me bypass all her other paramours, and I took that. I don't need to speak to Vienna everyday, I need to know that I'm valuable to her, and it thrills me to think that I am beyond subpar in her little black book. The space that I give her now will someday be equivalent to our success as a couple. Vienna souses herself in alienation, that's what she says, and I completely understand. But sometimes I'd like to be alone with just her.

Me: hey! I hope you're not dead!

An hour and a half pass by.

Me: okay! If you are dead, I am so sorry. Let me know you're okay!

12 minutes.

Me: vienna. please tell me that everything wasn't a lie…

20

I'm not one for social media, but I couldn't help but be curious. I simply needed to know if she was alive or okay. On one of her accounts, she posted that she would be going to a mini music festival this upcoming Saturday. She posted that forty-five minutes ago. Vienna doesn't even like live music, she told me that she keeps earplugs in at concerts because the consistent bass makes her nauseous. I checked her other account, and she posted a selfie two days ago with her cat, Media. Her cat was everything she wanted to be. I was confident that feeling would subside as long as I was in her life, she can radiate with my love. Vienna was slipping away, and I needed to take the necessary precautions to keep her.

Me: maybe it'll be better if we stop seeing each other. I really like you Vienna and I want to continue seeing you but this isn't going to work if you can't respond to a text.

Me: I'm sorry. I wish you the best of luck in all of your endeavors.

A one night stand would have sufficed. I'm okay with being someone's much-needed fuse box, and for Vienna, I could've been portable. All I needed, in the beginning, was an honest proclamation. I could've done without the sprinkled slander, and it would've served me better. I never second-guessed her intentions because I was certain that for once, I was given someone I deserve, and that I was rewarded for being a Good Samaritan. Vienna was the clearest depiction of a mental masterpiece. I forgot the number one rule of being an artist - paintings are never satisfactory, and a vision is never truly fulfilled.

Me: hi

Me: i miss you

Now I'm just pushing the puncture. I'm willing to see how far I can take this embarrassment, and how much more I can really mess this up. I've already revealed my persistency when it comes to her, and it was about time I unravel my integrity. At this point, I have nothing to lose because I've already lost her.

Me: tell me what I meant to you.
Me: you used me.
Me: and I let you.
Me: and i'd let you do it again.

5
The Sidelined
Gerry & Tob

GerrydaJew: how hard is it really?

GerrydaJew: i've always mistaken her for something that could stand in place of something else.

GerrydaJew: something that doesn't sting when it's pricked.

UDoneDidit: Were you the needle or the scab?

GerrydaJew: maybe I was both?

GerrydaJew: today I saw her sitting with cinth and I couldnt stop myself from thinking back. You know how white people put leashes on their kids?

UDoneDidit: You mean how YOUR ppl put leashes on their kids?

GerrydaJew: -__-

GerrydaJew: ya.

GerrydaJew: my thoughts of Vienna are the scatterbrained toddler

GerrydaJew: i've never been good at reeling things in.

UDoneDidit: I don't think anyone can reel her in

GerrydaJew: I dnot get it

GerrydaJew: one night her backside is scooped up against my abdomen

GerrydaJew: the next day she's holding hands with cinth

GerrydaJew: dont*

UDoneDidit: Damn

GerrydaJew: and theyre both extremely good looking

GerrydaJew: wtf

UDoneDidit: What does Cinth look like?

GerrydaJew: like a model dipped in milk

UDoneDidit: Non-fat or whole

GerrydaJew: coconut

UDoneDidit: isn't Vienna also dating Nolan?

GerrydaJew: who is also dating delilah

UDoneDidit: HAAAAA

UDoneDidit: Delilah is still there?

GerrydaJew: every

GerrydaJew: single

GerrydaJew: week

UDoneDidit: Did you get those mechs in the tunnel?

GerrydaJew: yup
GerrydaJew: i gotta load up on ammo anyway
GerrydaJew: and my pride

UDoneDidit: Word.

GerrydaJew: i dont get it
GerrydaJew: im a great guy
GerrydaJew: im a catch
GerrydaJew: i have a real job
GerrydaJew: unlike nolan who doesnt even have a place to live
GerrydaJew: physically I may be okay
GerrydaJew: but the way I feel about her never comes up short

UDoneDidit: I dont think it has anything to do with you
UDoneDidit: I think Vienna doesnt want to be loved

GerrydaJew: if you met her
GerrydaJew: you would know she does

UDoneDidit: It probably helps that I never met her
UDoneDidit: From what it seems her looks manipulate peoples psyche
UDoneDidit: People like that dont get off on others and then get over
UDoneDidit: They absorb others until they arent anything else
UDoneDidit: So glad Im a virgin.

GerrydaJew: Vienna is the third girl i ever hooked up with so I don't have much to compare it to
GerrydaJew: shes the best tho
GerrydaJew: shell always be the best

UDoneDidit: so this is what love looks like?

GerrydaJew: In one form, ya

UDoneDidit: Go get the dagger from Medidiya

GerrydaJew: shit
GerrydaJew: shiiiiiittttt

UDoneDidit: This is why I refuse to fall in love.
UDoneDidit: It screws with important business.

GerrydaJew: lol
GerrydaJew: pls shut up
GerrydaJew: hey Tob
GerrydaJew: do you have any pics of yourself on your laptop?
GerrydaJew: it'd be cool to finally see you

6
The Soul Identifier
Lora

I set up an email address because I thought it would be easier for her to contact me that way. That's not like Vienna though, she doesn't like to make things easy. So instead, she sketches out pictures of her time in New York City, intricate and involved doodles that speak louder than I've ever heard her talk. Sometimes I'll get ten to fifteen drawings in a row, and other days I'll be lucky to get a full page. She only calls me when she's in the mood, and Vienna is bare moods that like to overcompensate for her nonattendance. I would tell her I'm her sister, and that is enough to keep me stable, unlike her.

When my Aunt Yami told me Vienna was coming home for the weekend, I almost fell off the dining room seat. Vienna loves to stay away much too often, and she would always reassure me that she would be home soon, but the word *soon* is just a deferment. I had to ask my aunt over and over if it were true, if Vienna was really coming, and Aunt Yami said yes until she got annoyed and eventually left me at the table. I didn't care. I'd sit and wait at that table until I heard the sound of Vienna's keychain scrapping the apartment door. I wonder if I'm too big now to run and surprise-jump on her back like I always do. The last time I did it, she fell on top of her carryon, and my Aunt yelled at me for the entire period of Vienna's stay.

"*No la molestes*," she said. I didn't even know what that meant because Vienna and I don't speak Spanish, but Aunt Yami overflows with Spanglish.

I made sure to organize my wardrobe for Vienna to see because that was going to be the first thing I showed off. When Vienna and I were kids, we had about five outfits each, and every night, she'd be up late hand washing the clothes we wore that day. Our mom was busy, she wasn't there. Since living with Aunt Yami, I get to pick out my clothes, and I even own three pairs of Converse. My mother never bought us converse, not the name brand ones at least.

"Lora, *por favor*, **spanishspanish**," Aunt Yami screamed. She knows no other basses besides screaming.

"Vienna is going to be here soon, I don't have time to clean," I responded.

"That's your excuse to be lazy!" as Aunt Yami said this, I heard a light thump on the door. The sound caused Aunt Yami and I to stand in stillness. The anticipation of the stranger on the opposite end of the door made my palms shiver, even though I knew exactly who it was.

The duffle bag lead her through the door, and pretty soon, she was standing right beside the entrance. It's only been a couple of months since the last time I saw Vienna, but every first second seems like I'm holding in a mouthful of decades. Her hair was cut very short but still long enough to expose her curl pattern. She wore a violet-colored romper and a pair of white canvas shoes that weren't even dirty. Her legs are what I always thank God for because I knew they were coming in my near future. She looked a little startled by our immobility, but the distraught expression on her face welded into a smile.

"Hi Aunt Yami," Vienna dropped her bag and embraced Aunt Yami, who was already crying dry tears, then she looked at me. "Hi, Lora."

I was stunned. I couldn't control my wobbling knees. My fingers were clenching invisible bowling balls, and I was sure that if I let go of the feeling, my nerves will implode like pins. She looked beautiful. Vienna looked like someone I shouldn't know because they are beyond my frivolous fifteen-year-old world. I know they say that New York City changes people, but I never truly understood until the change nearly changed me. Vienna was my sister, but looking at her in this moment, I realized that Vienna was also becoming Vienna, or whoever that may be.

She didn't wait for me to make the first step. She relaxed her hands on my shoulders and drew me in. I could smell her perfume, and I could tell by the infrequent disposition of it that it was secondhand. We were almost the same height, but she was still tall enough to rest her chin on the top of my head, she swayed me from side to side, kissing my hair every couple of seconds. I couldn't see the expression on her face, but I knew that her eyes were closed, and she was thawing out in this moment. She couldn't see me, but she knew that my face saturated in tears.

"Vienna," was the only thing I could say.

Letting go wasn't on my agenda, but once Aunt Yami

heard the pent-up rumbles erupting from Vienna's stomach, we were both tugged into to the kitchen. The food wasn't done yet, and it was already half-past ten. Aunt Yami made a pot of rice and beans that could feed us for a week, and probably half the other families in the complex. Vienna and I sat across from each other at the table, exchanging faces full of repressed laughter because we knew that we'd be sitting here for another forty-five minutes. Aunt Yami would frenziedly adjust her apron that protected her against nothing because the food stains were already halfway down her t-shirt. Every so often, she'd turn and say,

"Are you ready to eat?" and even though we were, she was never ready to feed us.

"Do you need help, Aunt Yami?" Vienna asked nearly escaping her seat.

"*Sientate*. No! You are the guest this weekend. Vienna, you are going to die when you taste my pernil. Gustavo can't get enough of it!"

"Oh, I don't eat pork anymore," if only the wooden spoon in Aunt Yami's hand could talk.

"*Esta bien*. I'll make you chicken; do you want chicken?" I was surprised Aunt Yami was holding in the porkless-Vienna news better than I thought.

"It's okay Aunt Yami. I'll just have the rice and beans."

A couple moments of pure silence passed before our plates were in front of us. Aunt Yami began the mini feast with a prayer. I peeked to find Vienna complacently holding our hands, her head was upright, and her eyes gazed around the room. She caught my silent glance and grinned at me as if she was letting me know that it's okay to not do this. I turned away from her stare, and allowed my focus to fall down to my knees.

"How's New York, Vienna? **Spanishspanish**, you've been here for over an hour and said two words," Aunt Yami slammed a spoon full of rice into her mouth. Every time she did this, the excess skin under her arm would jiggle and make me laugh to myself.

"It's good. I like it."

"Are you ever thinking of moving back to Miami?"

"I don't think so," Vienna twirled her fork around in her food. She'd prick a bean and I'd watch it burst open onto the blade.

"Maybe Lora can live with you when she's done with High School. Her grades are so good, y'know? She can get a scholarship or something like that."

"Yeah, Lora is super smart," Vienna nudged my arm and winked.

I couldn't believe how pretty she had grown to be. It was like looking at a completely different person. I could tell by Aunt Yami's face that even she was surprised by Vienna's flowering beauty. Uncle Gustavo would go on and on about how beautiful Vienna was, and I would want him to shut up, but I could finally see it. Aunt Yami could see it too, which is why her next question was, "You got any boyfriends?"

"No."

"A beautiful girl like yourself should have a boyfriend or two. Back in my day, I had about seven boyfriends," Aunt Yami cackled and moved the small circular table. "Y'know, Lora has a boyfriend."

"I do not! Oh my God, Aunt Yami, stop!" I knew where she was going with this.

"He's so cute, he's a little black boy. *Ay que lindo*, you're just like your mother. Your mom used to always be with the black boys."

"He's not my boyfriend. He's just some boy in band with me," I took my first bite of the pernil. I wasn't sure if it was extremely dry, or if Vienna had already influenced my taste buds.

"What's his name?" Vienna was blushing at my embarrassment.

"Paris."

"You didn't tell me that! Oh man, he might be a little fruity-tooty," Aunt Yami directed a face at Vienna who dismissed it.

"I like that name," Vienna said. She stood up and placed her dish into the sink. "I think I'm going to get some sleep. Lora, mind if I sleep with you?"

Vienna took her shower before me, which made me want to skip bathing all together because I knew it would allow me to have more time with her. When I turned the shower-head on, I didn't even wait for it to get hot, I jumped underneath the brisk spritz, and allowed my hair to get wet enough to make someone believe I had a real rinse. My room was right next to the bathroom, and I could hear the guitars strumming from Vienna's phone, and it made washing up real soothing. I could also hear Vienna humming along to the singer's sound. Once the song was done, I knew it was time for me to get out.

I rubbed the fog off of my mirror to uncover my reflection. I poked at my round jaw and fluffed my cheeks that made my lips look ginormous. My hair curled down my back and puffed up at the top, making me look like I was hiding ears underneath. I wondered if I'd look good with a short haircut, something similar to what Vienna has. The more I looked at myself, the more I realized how much Vienna and I don't favor one another. I knew she was much older than me, but I wanted puberty to leave its everlasting fingerprints. I wanted to look like that. We share similar features, but Vienna's complimented her in ways I couldn't imagine them complimenting me. I can surely wish.

"That was fast," Vienna was spooning my pillow in an oversized dyed shirt.

"I took a shower right before you got here," I laughed. I was also lying. I sat on the edge of the bed, curling my legs up into a pretzel shape.

"You don't want to cuddle me? Too big for that now?"

Vienna giggled.

It's been so long since Vienna and I slept on the same bed together, the last time we did was with our mom. We would all crowd up in her full-sized bed, Vienna nearly falling off every time, and me wishing she would go away so my mom and I could have the entire mattress to ourselves. Vienna was never afraid of isolation. My mom would ritually face me, and I liked facing her because facing the opposite side made me think a monster was going to come out of her closet.

I crawled up onto the bed and laid my head on Vienna's thighs. This was something I used to do with my mom while she would talk on the phone and I pretended to watch TV. Even though I wasn't intentionally eavesdropping, my mom's chatter would cloud the room and request my attention. I never understood what she was talking about because I was too young to understand. Now I listen to Vienna who doesn't say much, but her blinks love to chitchat.

"Your hair is so long," I could feel Vienna's slim fingers separating my strands.

"Yeah. I thought about cutting it."

"Like mine?" Vienna asked.

"Yeah."

Vienna scooted down so that her face was directly in front of mine. She poked my nose and slid her finger up my bridge, and to my forehead. She elongated the rest of her fingers along my cheek like a spider stretching its limbs, and patting me. At first, I thought she was making fun of me, but her expression was endearing and focused. Any other moment, I would laugh at something like this, but there was a subtle intensity that Vienna emitted. There was a streak in her stare that made me want to look away but also let me know that it was okay to look further. It's just, I wasn't sure what I was looking into or who.

Aunt Yami said that Vienna was changing. I don't listen to Aunt Yami because she speaks nonsense most of the time, but I was starting to understand what she meant. I always knew Vienna was changing because she was no longer here in Florida, and she was transitioning into a new person. Aunt Yami said that Vienna was having problems, and that her mind was going raw. Aunt Yami didn't go further into details, and I never questioned it. Not even until now. I know Vienna's brown eyes, and I know them better than anyone else because they are my own. However, they don't reflect familiarity.

"You look beautiful, Lora," Vienna exhaled and closed her eyes. "You look just like mom."

7
The Wandering Sparrow
Topher

I used to see her all the time walking through Higgins. She never looks up when she walks, and I can tell she's sketching out blueprints of the hauled shoestrings in front of her. I know her heavy head isn't a confidence issue because when she does look up, her glances go unbroken. Our interactions have never been longer than a full breath, but they were notable to me.

I was so accustomed to her route that the Tuesday afternoon I didn't see her, I spent thirty minutes wandering the campus just to make sure nothing terrible happened. The following Tuesday was the same story, and every Tuesday after that was no different. I realized she wasn't going to come back. I resented myself never to get her name, and assumed I never would - it wasn't until that day.

I was sitting in the overpopulated coffee shop right outside my retail job. I hated the spot, but I didn't differ from the average New Yorker who sustained off of filthy bean water. I was listening to a podcast about an obscure television series while also fixing my freshly ruptured wristwatch. My days have never been great. Some construction guys gathered in front of me, each shooting bull with one another. They had a load of saran-wrapped bagels surging throughout the tiny table, and each time one of them would laugh, I'd await the suicide drop of one of the breaded brothers. Their voices were so booming that I found my index finger stapled to the sound button on my phone. I knew that I couldn't tell them to quiet down because I was about the size of one of their arms, but their voices soon came to an unexpected rest. A much-needed rest for me.

She always dripped in irresistibility, but this day, she was covered in want. The construction workers didn't know what to say, even their catcalling was mediocre to her actual existence. I could see the cashiers gleefully anticipating her arrival, and politely competing for her order. I turned off my phone because I didn't want anything to interrupt my view of her. I scuffled to the edge of my seat, my ear sticking out to hear what caffeinated delight would satisfy her this morning. Perhaps it wasn't a coffee she desired, maybe she was in the mood for something as decadent as the way she looked and went down as smooth as I'm sure she does. Her full lips lost one another, and her exquisite voice danced out. I wasn't quite sure if the cashier was equipped for a waltz, but who wouldn't camouflage their two left feet for her?

"A butter croissant, please," she said as she uncovered her cartoon decorated wallet. I wasn't sure what the animation was, but it was some kind of taupe bunny head. She's insanely perfect.

"Is that all?"

"Yes."

"May I have a name, please?" The barista was shivering in this woman's presence.

"Vienna."

If there was any name I could've guessed, it would have been Vienna. A lively city full of enchanting architecture and breath-stealing landscapes, I couldn't think of anything more befitting. The treacherous humid air had yet to hit New York this late Spring, but her outfit was already celebrating the sunny days. She wore a long flowing mahogany dress with ripples, and her short coils created waves around the structure of her face. I couldn't help but notice the bareness of her chest, and that was merely me being a guy. Even though her body wasn't giving in that department, I wanted so bad to grasp her bare torso in my palms.

Vienna spun around, scavenging for a seat. I could see a couple of people removing their property from vacant spaces, trying to free up a spot for the ravishing woman. It was hard to tell if she was interested in having a seat, but I was trying to fill it out before she made up her mind. I wanted to be her taker. Hell, I'll even treat her to a beverage. I wonder what kind of conversation I could brew up, or if she'll remember me. I knew there was a great chance that she wouldn't because people don't often recall the ones who question them on restroom directions. If she sits next to me, I'll immediately introduce myself to her, that would be appropriate. I couldn't let her get away this time without pushing my existence onto her. I wanted her to know that I'm alive, and that I'm here if she wants me.

The employee took too long to hand her the croissant, but once it was in her hand, the succeeding moment would determine our possible fate. Vienna crumbled the brown paper bag in her hand and proceeded toward the door, looking at her feet as always. I could hear some teenage boys muffling some stuff at her, and I considered calling the police to notify them about some school cutters. Before she was fully out the door, she staggered on some old woman's purse. Vienna's face read as apologetic, but she didn't verbally apologize. She looked up for a quick minute in minor humiliation, and that was when our eyes connected. My face was so chilled that I wasn't sure if I was smiling or viciously gawking.

We looked at each other for a bit. I could tell that everyone in the cafe was witnessing what I was experiencing, and I hoped someone was recording the moment. I wasn't sure why, but I was standing up, and I couldn't tell why Vienna's stumble caused my body to jolt upward. It was as if she was waiting for me to say something. I didn't know what to say. I was waiting for this moment and reenacted this scenario in my head for the past few months, I thought i'd be more comfortable. The ideal setting had been created for us, I just had to make a move.

8
The Nurturer

Shannon

I could tell she was lying to me when she said she had prior babysitting experience. Whenever I questioned her about her little sister, she would defer the question. At first, this was a huge red flag, especially to a brand-new mom such as myself. My husband totally rejected her interview, but I soon convinced him that she was the ideal candidate. There was something spectacular in the way she looked at me. I knew that she came from a place, where that place was was a question I don't think I'll ever have answered. Even though her babysitting experience may have been a built-up fabrication, I was willing to let my guard down for Vienna. I needed to become comfortable with various transitions, especially since I recently had the biggest transition in my life extracted out of me.

I didn't leave Vienna's side during her first week, okay maybe the first month. I had to supervise every process because she wasn't a mom, and even though I can teach her how to warm a bottle, I can't teach her how to care for my child. I know that care converts into many things, but I'm referring to care in the rawest form. I wanted to know if Vienna was capable of caring for my child the same way I care for my child. I was even nitpicking the way she looked at Evelyn right before placing her into the crib. I needed to know if this job was more than just an easy buck. I've interviewed many nannies, and each one had a compiled list of achievements that meant nothing to me. I couldn't give a damn if someone had four children, all-natural births, and breastfed each one until they were two years old. I needed to know if they cared about my own baby as their own.

It was the first night I was leaving Vienna alone with Evelyn. My husband's company was hitting a huge milestone, and as a result, it forced all significant others to be present; some paid and some unpaid. As tentative as I was about Vienna, I honestly had no other choice but to place my child under her administration and care. Of course, I took the necessary extremities to oversee her every movement, and I must admit that the discreet camera was well worth $120. All four of them. I couldn't confess to my husband about my purchase because he would assume I was being neurotic, but the only thing he contributes to Evelyn's upbringing is a black credit card. There is nothing wrong with being a caring mother.

My phone was the only acquaintance I cared to make that night, and all the other housewives seemed far too vapid for a meaningful conversation. I could smell my husband's disapproval from across the table, and I wasn't going to give him the meekness he so passively demanded. I couldn't understand how any adult could sit in this ridiculously large room, only to drink champagne from an underpaid server, and chat about expensive past times while their children were at home with God knows who. I couldn't fall into that disorderly line. Instead, I continued to nosedive into my phone and block out all mangled gestures.

I don't know what I was looking for; perhaps, I hoped to find something I could run with. Something that would prove my husband right, which would make me seem like I'm too forgiving. I watched Vienna for hours. I watched her for so long that the minute the CEO gave the closing speech, I was in disbelief. I discovered nothing. Vienna cuddled Evelyn, fed her at all the correct times, read her book about the disobedient crayons, played with those organic blocks I got for her, put her to sleep, and she kissed her goodnight. When Evelyn woke up again, Vienna rushed to the room in less than ten seconds, and held her as though she carried her for nine months. Vienna did prove me wrong, not in the way she disappointed me, but she proved my parenting wrong.

"What's the matter?" my husband squeezed my shoulder in the backseat of the taxi.

"Nothing."

"I should've told you this before we left, but you look fantastic tonight," he placed his hand beneath my jaw and slowly rotated my head toward him. "It's nice to have a night without the baby. Hopefully, we can continue the night when we get back in."

"Did it cross your mind at all tonight if Evelyn was okay?"

"What do you mean?" The taxi halted at a stop sign, and the street lights outlined my husband's face.

"It's just, you didn't mention her all till now. She's been with a stranger all night."

"Of course, I thought about her. She's my child. I also thought about you, but you've been glued to your phone all evening. You're always cooped up in the house, I thought a night out would do you some good."

"I'm not a dog, I don't bark as soon as my leash is untied," we were two blocks away from the building. I unbuckled my seatbelt to prepare myself to bolt out of the car.

I checked my phone one more time before exiting. Vienna sat up on the sofa watching some reality television show, when I swiped over to Evelyn's screen, who was still fast asleep. I had to test her, though. I shot a quick text to Vienna, letting her know that we should be there in five minutes. I scurried back to the screen of her sitting down watching the television. I watched her pick up her phone, type something, then place her phone to the side of her thigh. I could see from the notification that she typed '*okay,*' with a smiley face. I waited to see if something would happen if she would bulge a bit or frantically try to do anything. She didn't, not even a little.

"Shannon, get out of the car," my husband stood in front of me, holding the door open with one hand, and reaching the other side out to escort me from the vehicle.

"Finally!" I exhaled and sped toward the building. I could see the doorman already stepping out of his booth to grab the door. I quickly swung the glass open, wide enough so that my husband can follow me in if he wanted to.

"Ms. Baiocchi," he smiled as I rang for the elevator door. "Mr. Baiocchi."

"Good evening." My husband muttered.

I had to let her go. I knew it started here, but this was only the beginning of a domino effect that my family couldn't succumb to. I created this family. I bared this surname name with all that was in me, and I wasn't going to allow some cute twenty-year-old destroy that. It starts off with building a relationship with the child, and slowly dribbles to the husband. Next thing I know, I'm going to discover her undergarments buried in my sheets. I wasn't sure the kind of act she was pulling, but I couldn't allow it. It could cause me to lose my place as a respectable parent, and that's all I had going for me right now. Vienna, I'm sure is perfect to many people, but I'm not looking for perfection. I'm looking for someone who cares.

9
The Mixer
Nolan

"Here?" her pelvis cowered over my legs, and her head hung toward my shoulder.

"Yeah," was her exhaled breath, fishing into my wandered off esophagus.

"You're so crazy," my lip was quenched at the possibilities of what was yet to come.

The puce sky hovered over us, and I'm pretty sure it locked us into a corner. Stellar. Vi's body drooped over me with curls that eclipsed the sun. We had a tone, but the couple next to us had no desire of masking their resentment; we two black folks being too damn loud. Deep down inside, they wanted to get with us, and Vi would be down for that sort of thing. She's down for anything. The grass was so damp, and my skin didn't like the contact, it woke me up too much. My exhilaration liked to propel through my body and decorate a dream. The dusk wanted to accompany me just a little longer, and my mind was crowd surfing through the clouds.

Vi is fun, she doesn't know consequences and balances on the unknowing. I forget with Vi, and that's why I swell in everything she is, in moderation. I descend into her world and pump my blood full of her muddy righteousness. That's when I forget about myself. Sometimes I fight with the strings of my guitar because my hands want to create music specifically about her. I can never predict the outcome of my melodies, especially when my thoughts are following to a distinct cadence. With Vi, I have to become my own parent and discipline myself, make sure that I stay grounded enough that I can recognize my own forsaken demise. Vi and I come from the same crumbling world, so I remind myself that fun can be had when the crumbles beg to be dust.

"Take off my panties," she dove further into me, her tongue peeking through her lips and linking onto mine.

I slid my hand up her thigh and under her dress. I quickly noticed the absent fabric across her rear, and promptly grabbed a handful of cheek. She liked this, I know that because she bit my tongue with her teeth, it hurt, but I wanted her to do it again. I felt her fingers draping downward until she met the zipper of my shorts. Vi pinched the small metal and drew it south. Her soft touch slipped in, and a massive gasp erupted from my mouth. I looked around to see if that couple noticed us, and of course they did, and they were preparing to flee the scene. I aligned my back with the bark, and correctly planted myself in the moment.

Love can exist here. Whatever infatuations derived from the enticing look in her eyes, it can all become stagnant. I give it permission to be. I don't believe in love, but I'm falling victim to this because it widens my unforgiving senses. Whether I'm genuinely whole with Vi was up to my brief discretion, can I be complete for these five minutes? Maybe not, but I can be greedy. I wasn't sure where Vi stood, but I was waving my arms at temporary enlightenment. My mind was sprinting and meditating, all at once. Love may not be real, but it can accompany me any day it wanted to, for right now.

"Vi," I gulped. I wasn't sure how much I could restrain myself.

She drew her head back, and glued the point of her nose to mine. We stared at each other as she swayed on top of me and caught her breath every minute she came down. I wanted to look into her and extract all the words that she can't say out loud. Her faint moans were ripe and fulfilling, but I wasn't getting enough from her. My hands became vines growing against her spinal cord, and I hooked onto her shoulders to bring her in a bit more. The measurement of her voice didn't change, but her eyes simply told me everything. I allowed gravity to continuously bring her to me, and she had no problems flowing with the laws of motion.

"I'm getting close," Vi grunted.

"Not yet, wait fo-"as the words escaped my mouth, she shriveled up into herself and collided into my embrace.

A few tender vibrations emitted from her body before she became completely still. I sat on the opposite end of what seemed like a second, trying to disentangle our ties. I could feel her regain the consciousness that I never ripped away from her, and fumble off to the side. I looked down at my stiff pride, attempting to decipher my notability. I couldn't force it to go down, and I had no interests baring it all in Prospect Park. I tucked it behind my disheveled briefs, and watched the bulge knock on my jean shorts. Vi was so lost in self-fulfillment that she nearly eradicated my entire existence. I knew I could make her feel good, but that was where my significance fell short, I didn't do anything. Vi didn't need me to make her feel good.

"That was nice," she placed her hand on my chest, kissing the side of my face.

"Glad I can help."

"Can't wait for tonight," she was glistening.

"Tonight?"

"Yeah, I'm taking you home with me."

"I can't tonight," I answered.

Vi and I are similar, and maybe that's why I swallow her in intervals. Coming from a place like CEASE where everyone is accessorized in their own catastrophes, it's easy to dismiss the crowd or become a product of it. Vi is made up of alternative components, not the same stuff that CEASE is used to. She's complicated. I noticed this from the minute I saw her, and when she spoke, I was transfixed. I never encountered someone who was like me or encompassed who I didn't want to be all in one. Vi is messed up, I see it in the rhythms of her voice and her choice of words. I'm sure that if Vi could doodle out the complexity of her thoughts, it would translate into a series of coils that ended nowhere. I don't know the person that can terminate that cycle, I'm not stable enough for that.

"Why?" was her question.

"I have to record some stuff with my drummer, we're almost done with this album."

"Can you come by after?"

"I may be able to sneak away," I could feel the buzz on my back pocket. I didn't have to check my phone to know it was Dell, Vi's parallel.

"You're not going to come, are you?"

Vi was intuitive. As fun as she was, she was also fiery. I can hook up with most women and simply let it be what it was, a temporary yet memorable experience, but not with Vi. Vi can be extremely shallow on most days, seek out pleasure for what it is, and live on that satisfaction. On other days, Vi is seen analyzing every breath, every quick glimpse, each minor delay to a question. She is undressing it. I know this was all a part of her symptoms, a result of her traumatic and voluntary anxiety. I knew many people who suffered from the disorder, but I've met no one with Vi's case. Vi can be the greatest person in the world, and to a great extent, her looks undoubtedly help with that. She can also maul someone for answers as to why she is empathetically paralyzed.

"Vi, let's just have fun right now."

I knew that even if she agreed, she was going to revolve around my decision to decline. Her head could be seen on mountain peaks, and her mind spits out negative suggestions like weighted avalanches. I couldn't be stuck behind that. Vi plays with people just as messed up as her because we aren't able to anatomize our relationships, whether disastrous or becoming. My bipolar likes Vi, but it also retracts. When my depression comes around, I am crippled from the thought of her. When I'm in that mindset, I can't be anything, and Vi wants everyone to be everything for her. We're both kind of selfish in different ways.

PART

TWO

Vienna

10
Sundown after Meteors
Cinth

My parents told me that love can always be traced. I never knew what they meant by that, but it seemed to be one of their few profitable conjoined quotes. I am the result of sonnets and intentional sentence fragments. My parents graciously gloat about their success as working writers, though they truly don't need to because the academic world does enough of that for them. Each have their own credible novels, along with one best-selling collaboration outlining my childhood. My mother always scorns my father and tells him how they should've waited to publish the book, at least waited long enough for me to fully come out.

I was born with female reproductive organs, but I always thought they were a waste, that someone else could use these. Not only was I extremely uncomfortable in everything that was pigeonholed as feminine, I snarled at the thought of my own name, Cynthia. Whenever I would hear that name, I was placed in front of an attenuated reflection of myself. I knew that I wasn't Cynthia, but I also knew that I wasn't a Charles or Christopher. I was just me. At an underdeveloped stage, I figured that I either had to be one or the other, I couldn't just be. I lived in that phase for a while, right up until I moved to New York.

NYU was not where I fully realized myself, not at all. I

realized who I was when Jakoda Fowler kissed me in the back seat of his mother's car while also honking my breast. Dowsing myself in black clothes was not me paying homage to all that is goth, it was just me being afraid to wear anything, and not sincerely conforming to the stigma that colors are. I internally chanted when I noticed that puberty was over, and my breast will never create a hefty silhouette behind tees. I wore hoodies to conceal my butt-touching blonde hair until I cut it all off in the eleventh grade, and I never allowed it to sprout again. I went into college having a better idea of who I was. I wasn't Cynthia, I was Cinth.

"Oh wait, you're a girl?" the common question I was asked right after second base had been annihilated.

"I just," was the only thing I could conjure up for a long time. My parents were writers, so I should be able to eloquently express my sexuality, but who am I?

What am I?

I met Leon where a friend of mine was hosting a performance piece at an art space in Fort Greene. The work itself had no characters, but it was clear who had the more prominent roles, and Leon was the centerpiece. It was effortless to find myself attracted to her because her glossy body was exposed the entire show. Her hair was longer than what mine used to be, and compiled of many stringy curls. At the end of the presentation, all the actors came forward to bow. Leon's hair threw back, and I had zero doubts that the stage lights flashed off her skin and made her glow. I didn't question whether or not I was going to bring her home with me. I had to.

"Why don't you take off your shirt?" she asked while slinking down my stomach.

"I don't ever take it off," I croaked as she unbuttoned my trousers. Here it comes.

"Do you shower in it too?" she giggled. I could see her pupils draw toward my sunken boxers.

"I'm...I just d-" before I could actually finish my sentence, she created a pair of scissors with her fingers, and opened up the slit. Her head bobbed forward, and I felt a moist coolness graze me.

"Huuuh!" the suddenness startled me, and I jerked upward. "What are you doing?"

"You don't like being eaten out?" she teehee'd.

"It's not that. I just...I never had someone touch *that* before," after I said this, Leon's face knotted around.

"*That?*" in a matter of seconds, Leon's entire aura altered. It was as though she had read the book that my parents wished they wrote, the book that told the real story of who I was. "What does your body mean to you?"

"I don't understand that question."

"No, you do understand, you don't want to answer."

Leon laid by my side for the rest of the night, most people

I hook up with end up leaving before the sun came up, but not her. It was hard to sleep, but it was easy to watch her. Her skin looked even better when dawn emerged and tickled her pores. I thought I was watching the construction of a real-life oil painting. Her naked breasts were pressed up against my rib cage, her butt hitting the wall. I wanted to wake her up while she dreamt in my arms, and ask her how can she be so confident. I wanted to know If my academically rich parents failed to teach me something down the line, and that's why I'm so messed up now.

I knew I would have to face this question at some point, not for Leon, but for my own special grace. I figured my body meant nothing to me, stirring thoughts that I could disregard and continue strolling down my falsehood. I couldn't sleep with the idea of Leon's lips stripping down the barriers that I manifested. It felt good. I never wanted anyone to reveal who I was to me, especially since I couldn't understand myself.

"Hi," I heard her purr into the a.m air.

"Hey," I didn't know whether or not I should kiss her.

"Cinth."

"Yes?"

"I'm gonna be real, I didn't know what you were," that seems to be the case for most people. "I just knew you were the best-looking person I've seen in a long-long time."

"Thanks, Leon."

"You should know that your body is yours, it is no one else's answer," her auburn eyes caressed me."But you should know what it means to you."

I wanted to kick Leon out so that I could weep in solitude. I attempted to veil the swift tear that dropped from my eyelash, but she was too quick at catching. She kneeled up and straddled me, her arms wedding around my neck. The stage lights flattered her well, but nothing could compare to the radiance of morning time. I wanted to collect my tears, but they gathered at the brim of my top lip, along with the running snot from my nose. I didn't know why I was crying. I couldn't pin-point the moment where I convinced myself that it was okay not to. Leon resurrected these emotions that passed away years ago.

I wouldn't say that Leon jump-started my full transition, but she was the nudge to an awakening. I met some of Leon's friends, some who were like me, and some who identified as trans. It took me some time to really put who I was into words, but I always explained it as, I am my most authentic self, and who that is is not defined. I am Cinth, not she or he, I am Cinth. I know that I'm attracted to women, I know I like the feeling of receiving cunnilingus, and I know that I go into the men's bathroom to piss. The more I walked around believing myself, the more I abandoned the need to explain. I was finally living.

My junior year in college, I decided that it was time to reintroduce myself to my parents. I took the bus home to Norristown for the weekend, and my confession recoiled from the tinted Greyhound glass, and back onto my lap for the entire 4 hours. The second I stepped through my front door, my words stumbled out of me and scuffed up my parent's floors. It was like I

56

was waiting years for this encounter, and since I had a starting motive, I could only see my actions through. I didn't well up because I was sure of myself. I wasn't necessarily hankering for my parent's approval either, I was inviting them to my revival.

"Cinth, the obvious thing for me to say would be to tell you that we knew the entire time, and of course we did. We knew who you were," my mom removed her marigold glasses from her face and created a headband with them. "We were waiting for *you* to know who you are."

My dad stood by the entrance of the basement with a cardboard box in his hand, he always had projects in his hands, and continuously nodded, "I'm not saying you need a therapist, but it could be beneficial to talk to a professional about your new-found discovery. You may want to do that before you are no longer covered under our health insurance."

"I don't think I'll need that, but thanks."

I didn't think I would. Not at the time. After I graduated college, that was when the striking torches started to really blaze. Many companies have a non-discriminatory policy, but still forced applicants to list their gender. I felt no need to comply with those rules, and my parents being who they are, encouraged me to never bend for corporate expectations. That idea seemed liberating, that was until I found myself waiting tables, and scavenging for nickels and dimes to pay my New York City rent. My questions started to arise again, my imaginary need to conform to something, to fit in, it all began to precipitate through me. I didn't want to admit to the help, but I needed it, I needed to speak to a professional because I needed someone to help me stay grounded in my own shoes.

Finally, I met with a therapist, and after a few sessions, they told me about CEASE.

People go into group therapy with no expectations because the full range of personalities could produce anything, so the only hope is to really understand the issue therefore to communicate it verbally. I was going into group therapy while trying to re-find myself, so I went in with all the expectations in the world. But I never thought that I would see her.

She was sitting perpendicular to myself, and her eyes were fixed to me like they were always broken; we were in group therapy, so I knew they were. Everyone outwardly introduced themselves except for her, she knew that the sight of her was all the introduction that I needed. My parents told me that love can always be traced, and I didn't know what that meant, I didn't know until I was led to Vienna.

11
To Fly from Concrete
Karishma

Vienna was the girl in kindergarten who stuck her index finger into the mechanical sharpener. I was standing next to her when this happened, frolicking in nothing but good intentions, and depraved nap time. I recall the complete insertion, and the look on her face when she removed the slashed finger from the contraption. The nail hadn't snatched off completely, half of it remained intact, and the other half throbbed in dubiety.

Her hair was always parted in thick braids with colorful barrettes at the end, and I distinctly remember one of them falling simultaneously as her finger became fully exposed. At first, Vienna didn't react, her eyes floated over the wound and onto me, who shuddered at the mere sight. When the barrette finally hit the floor, Vienna broke out in a vicious yelp. The teacher scurried over in panic, and studied the severity of the injury. I knew all that went through Mrs. Bradley's mind was, why would this child stick her hand into a sharpener?

There were two boys in our class, Brandon Cadwell and Jared Cadwell, they were cousins. Vienna had the biggest crush on Jared, as big as her five-year-old self could emote. Jared wasn't the more physically desirable one of the two, Brandon was, he had the smile. Even though Vienna wanted Jared, she hopscotched back and forth between both of them. I was standing beside her in line, which was something I often did since we were the same height, and everything was based on gradual elevation in elementary school; that was when Vienna began to convey her plans to me before heading on our school trip.

"Kari, I'm going to sit next to Jared on the way there, and you have to sit next to Brandon because I don't want anyone else sitting next to Brandon," she said. "On the way back, we're going to switch."

Later on in the year, Vienna's mom threw a party in the classroom for her birthday. All the kids liked going up to Vienna's mom because she was pretty and sweet. She was wearing a pair of jeans that accentuated her butt, but not in a suggestive way. Edgar Hernandez tapped me on my thigh, and told me that Vienna's mom was hotter than her because she was whiter than her. I found that comment to be superfluous, but I didn't expect much from him or any of the other kids in our class. Vienna's mom was strikingly beautiful, but it had nothing to do with her complexion. Vienna also wasn't hot, but she shouldn't be at that age. At the end of the party, Vienna ran to her mom, throwing her compact body onto her mother's shoulders, and they embraced until it was time to clean up. I remember the way Vienna hugged her mom, she hugged her mom as if she didn't know her mom.

Vienna and I moved onto first, second, and third grade together. We promised each other that we would be best friends forever. Vienna would always come to my house, and we both would make fun of my sister, Bhavya, who was a paragon of preteen existence. Vienna and I would memorize different ballads from famous Bollywood movies, and present them to my family.

My mother and grandmother were always impressed by how well Vienna could speak Hindi, I was a hard-ass with her though. I would lie and tell her that if she uttered a word incorrectly, she was actually making a nasty comment in my language. Vienna never wanted to offend anyone. That was the kind of person she was.

In the middle of third grade, I told Vienna that I was moving to California. Vienna had a hard time getting along with the other students in third grade, I wasn't really sure why, but she started to become more and more closed off. Since she neglected her need to make more friends, she assumed that I would do the same, and that caused friction within our innocent relationship. Secretly, I was well excited to move to a different state, but I couldn't tell Vienna about that. I encouraged her to call me, and that she could come visit whenever she wanted, but I knew as soon as I said that, she wasn't going to. I didn't want to come to full terms with it, but something had gone missing in Vienna since I met her, it was all too grown up for me to understand. It was too grown up for her.

12
To Fondle an Egg
Chad

Vienna was well aware of the birds and the bees, I double-checked. She was wildly unearthly, and we all knew it, we just ha-ha'd it off. She had a stuffed lassie named, Margo that she carried everywhere she went. The thing secreted toddler breath, and whatever smells that come from a nine-year-old. She was always squirming when she sat down, and I figured maggots were dominating her embryonic vag.

Vienna herself hated taking baths, but spent an unusual amount of time in the restroom, and I knew she wasn't pissing. She liked to pee everywhere but the toilet. Whenever she slept over, we had to layout the same pads on the bed that we used for the dogs, but she peed so much that it would leak through. Vienna's mom started to resent her during this time, while constantly comparing her to her cousin of the same age, my little sister. So, Vienna spent most of the time at our house because her mother was nowhere to be found.

I was exterminating Madeline in Tekken, who was fourteen, a year older than me, while Vienna was in the corner playing with some naked-ass doll. She had on a pair of worn-out lime underpants, and a white t-shirt that had her name written in multicolored cursive. Her shirts were always too small for her, and that was cause her mom never took her shopping. I forgot what Madeline was talking about, but it all ended up with me blowing her off and going over to Vienna. Vienna's hair was stupid long and never combed, about seventy percent of it was knots and tangles. I picked up one of her forgotten dolls, who was also naked and moved his legs around to make him do splits.

"Ow! My balls! Ow! My balls!" I banged him against the floor while his legs were entirely separated.

"Chad, don't," she snatched the dude away from me. I laughed because she was only half bothered.

Vienna stood up and made her way into the closet. That was her favorite place to hang out in my house, and I found it spooky that someone of her age wasn't afraid of the dark, my sister damn sure was. Most of the time, I left her alone, went on about playing my game with Madeline, but I thought maybe I'd give her some attention for once.

I joined her in the closet and found her leaning up against a pile of disintegrating textbooks. Vienna was huddled up at the peak of the stack, and I could see her brown eyes emanating toward me. I trekked further back and sat beside her. She didn't scoot to provide me with more sitting space, instead, she sat stationary while our legs touched.

We sat in silence until I decided to reach my hands under her armpits, and judder my fingers underneath her. Vienna didn't like being tickled, but she didn't stop me. I continued to do this as she pressed her back against the wall, and held her breath so that she wouldn't laugh. Which was an odd thing to do because there's nothing wrong with having fun. She started to return my movements, energetically tickling me, which inevitably made her squeak with giggles. She pushed forward and our chests bumped. Vienna was young, but she was developing quickly, and faster than my sister, for sure. Vienna had tits.

"Do you know what sex is?" I questioned her. She sat back, as bashfulness swarmed through her cheekbones.

"Yeah," she answered.

"Do you want to do that?" she hesitated; even though it was pitch-black, I could see her cat-like stare wander down and back up to me.

"No."

13
The Sweat of a Prophet
Delilah

I can't taste impious acidity, but I'm sure it stanks more than the underbelly of the devil. I'm confident that it probably leaks too, and catches fire when it comes in contact with a meritorious flame. I always pray that fixed idealizations soon stride long enough to walk into the punctured arms of my Lord and Savior, Jesus Christ.

These people are nothing but festered taints that emerge from carnal diseases. These people, people like Vienna, blossom in the coolest of climates because they are only a manifestation of their befouled selves. There are so many nomadic souls whose faith become prolonged due to feral and inconsiderate distractions. There is nothing that can be done once the soul has dwelled, I can only lift my praying hands to the righteous and beg for a successful extraction.

Amen.

The backyard pool was the only project my mama could swing her pennies into, and it made her feel important. She tried to get me to swim in that wasteful water since I scuba dove out of her lady bit. I couldn't muster up the paragraphs of repugnance and detestation that I inhibited at a young age, and if I could, I'd spit them in her face to watch them decontaminate her fleeting intellect. That liquid was cursed. I ripped a sheet from the bible, threw it in, and watched it decompose right in front of my eyes in less than a second. I could only assume what that toxicity would do to me, probably unsheathe the word directly from my core, and manipulate it with its whirl.

My brother, Zeke only swam in the water because he knew it would satisfy mama, he's a nuisance for that. Zeke was a real mama's boy, his mouth replaced her pocket mirror whenever she was missing it. He persistently claimed that all the boys in school were smitten by her walk, and they were going to start a riot in Lexington for her attention. I shunned Zeke ever since that sentence riddled from his cracked teeth, he should know better than to lie under the eyes of the Lord. Zeke was always the fool, and I was always trying to keep him from getting the foolishness beaten out of him. It was a good thing that I was a catch, and it benefitted him to have me as his twin, that way I could keep a close eye if need be.

"Delilah, why do you hate mama?" my parents penalized my existence by forcing me to share a room with my brother.

"I don't hate her," I detested.

"You don't look at her with kind eyes."

"Shut up. I'm trying to get some sleep."

I promised myself that one day, I would drive down to South Carolina, and pawn each church hat my mother owned. If it weren't for her need to over- exaggerate our finances, I wouldn't be looking at student loan debt till my skin turns to the texture of paper bills. My daddy told me that I should be more accepting, stating that my mama made many sacrifices during my childhood, and I should express an equal amount of gratitude to her that I do to Jesus. That was the most foul statement my father had ever made. Jesus Christ submitted himself for me to live freely, my mother wears the parent label to dictate respect. If my vision is ever so bright, she is wholly indebted to *me*.

My daddy purified the pool himself the day I was diagnosed with OCD. He told me that any child of his would be able to scrub off a mental ailment, and arise from the water rejoiced in newfound glory. I never wanted to mortify my daddy like that; he held this family, specifically me, in high regard. It wasn't like I could lie about it because the disease was fixed to my speech, and it drugged my reasoning. The contorted ideas came first, the ticks then accompanied everything else. My teachers confronted my parents without my consent, and looped them into an iniquitous conversation about my needs. I was reduced to an idea of myself that everyone held but me, and my parents shipped me to one of the most noteworthy psychiatrists in town.

"I thought OCD was when people need to turn the lights on and off, stuff like that," my daddy insisted.

"Delilah has that to a minimal degree, but she has intrusive and contaminated thoughts."

"What does that mean, what does that have to do with this thing?" my stupid mother asked.

"It means Delilah obsesses over people in an unhealthy

way. She has an ongoing string of thoughts about a person, it becomes a burden for her to complete daily tasks, or to focus at all."

This doctor's wife didn't love him. I could see the pulled in skin that ruptured on his ring finger, and the way he tried to distract people with his fancy profession. Mama was attracted to him though, she liked anything that still held onto its hair, and this man had a ponytail. I was happy that they left Zeke in the car because this detection would've done no good for him. I had to protect Zeke too, even if I had to protect him from myself. The doctor told me that if side effects arise, I would need to swat them faster than a gnat, luckily I'm immune to repercussions.

"Delilah, what is Luke 6:45?" My daddy held me by the shoulders.

"*The good man out of the good treasure of his heart brings forth what is good; and the evil man out of the evil treasure brings forth what is evil; for his mouth speaks from that which fills his heart.*"

"You're a good one Delilah, I know this because you're my daughter."

Everybody was worried about me moving to New York City after college, they thought it'd turn me into one of those train moles, but that was all myths. I promised I'd still walk in the footsteps of faith, and if I trip, at least I know I'm always falling into familiar hands.

I got a job offer from an all-girls school in Brooklyn, the good part of Brooklyn. My mama said that I need to go wherever the faces are so bright they can guide me back to my apartment. My daddy had to correct her and console me all at the same time, she's such trouble. My daddy flew with me to New York and cosigned my apartment in Prospect Heights. I was thankful to have him by my side during my move because leaving him behind would buffer my transition. My daddy is the closest thing to a living embodiment of the Lord that I have, so I keep him close.

The school had a distinct policy, none of the students are graded, or given exams. Each child *should* be graded, we are ranked in life, and we are competing for unspoken standards. That's why I gobble down medication, to make me socially suitable. This made-up academic structure was pulled out of the toe pus of some flower-licking hippy parent, who inherited enough funds to run a school. Children should be competing for acknowledgment through their merits, and not their popularity. When kids are given the freedom to challenge an institution, it turns into a debacle of backwash. I would never scorn a child, but there's one student who wouldn't understand modesty if it hung in-between the creases of her braid.

"Miss. Gibson, I just don't get it. Why am I the one in trouble?"

"You're in trouble because you and seven other girls verbally attacked Tonya," this school was an embarrassment to my entire adult career. They encouraged teachers to have conversations with students instead of reprimanding them.

"I feel attacked that you are misjudging my constructive feedback toward my peer."

"It isn't your job to give constructive feedback, it's mine."

"I'm sorry Miss. Gibson, I thought it was your job to teach math and to criticize anything that pertains to that subject."

I reached my hand inside of my desk while still preserving eye contact with the clouded vemen that Aurora was. The wooden case stubbed my finger, and I dragged it out of its shaded quilt. I dropped it onto the top of the desk, and Aurora's eyes couldn't find their equilibrium. Her lips frazzled apart, and her face looked as though a dog had just defecated on this very table. I unlocked the enclosed case, and lifted up the Bible with both of my palms, as though I was picking up a batch of freshly mined gold and no one could tell me it's not.

"What are you doing?" Aurora started to cave into her seat, her fingertips carved into her exposed pink thighs.

"First Peter 5:5, *Likewise, you who are younger, be subject to the elders. Clothe yourselves, all of you, with humility toward one another, for God opposes the proud but gives grace to the humble.*"

"I don't think you can do this."

"First Timothy 3:11, *In the same way, the women are to be worthy of respect, not malicious talkers, but temperate and trustworthy in everything.*"

"I'm leaving! You can't do this!" Aurora jumped from her seat.
"Shut up and sit down!" I startled her. Good. Even though Aurora's heels were facing the door, this was the only time I've ever seen that child obey authority.

It was on a Monday afternoon when I told Aurora that she had to listen to me because I was speaking for our Father. On Wednesday, the principal approached me, and informed me that my final day would be that Friday. The hippy then went on to hand me pamphlets on self-care. I discarded them all under her nose and trotted out. The following week I received a phone call from someone named Ross telling me about his program, he said to me that a dear friend of mine recommended me to his therapy group. I told Ross that I don't have any friends. His voice was feathery and rang through my phone so much that I thought I was getting another call.

"Delilah, I'd love it for you to come," I figured the church could pluck any thorn to dagger, but my daddy convinced me that a change could be necessary. God put Ross in my life for a reason, and that was to follow his path.

I arrived before everyone that first morning, even before Ross himself. The room was kept in the corner of an old community center in Queens. The chairs were all scuffed up, and a net of profanity swung over all of them. I went around the room, reorganizing the seats in what I assumed was once a circle. A stack of blank name tags sat at the edge of a table, I took one, and drew my name out in the finest cursive one could see.

"Nothing compares to unfiltered honey grazing the palate of someone who was once sweet," a man took the seat right beside me.

I could tell by the depth of his voice that it wasn't Ross. When he looked directly at me, I whispered a quick prayer under my breath and noticed the loose hair on his beard. He was never someone I would look twice at in Lexington, not for the same reason. But here, here he was an array of delectable testimonies. His eyes steered down to my name tag and the side of his mouth curved upward.

"Wouldn't you say, Dell?"

14
Within Another Plain
Wyatt

There are but so many girls that can look at a flowing leaf and chase it. Vienna was one of those girls. The kind of girl that meshes with the crowd well, but holds enough independence to defend her identity. Vienna was never explanations that play-fought with her existence, she was an underdone hypotheses. I didn't need an origami fortune teller to tell me that Vienna was going to be my best friend, that was something that couldn't have been avoided. As pretty as Vienna was, our relationship never progressed passed platonic. It was an unspoken agreement between the two of us, and I'd agree to it a million times more.

If I were as artistically gifted as Vienna, I would quit all things that are related to school. I would persuade my parents to invest in my isolated art cabin in the woods, that way, I could produce thousand dollar paintings all day. Though Vienna's sketches are far beyond her modest descriptions of them, I knew she would never be able to devote her life to just art.

Vienna and I come from very different backgrounds, she didn't talk about hers too much, but she talked about it enough for me to have an understanding. I paint from the inspiration that I get from others. I can paint a realistic portrait of a homeless man and capture the despair in his eyes down to his soiled clothing, but that's just good. Vienna expresses her unuttered words in her drawings, she says things in her work that can't be told in person, and that's what really touches people. Everyone liked Vienna at school, especially Mrs. Talken.

"You all can learn something from Vienna," Mrs. Talken stood smack dab in the middle of the room. Everyone was looking beyond their easels, and Vienna was sitting off to the far left of the room, her face hidden behind her batch of curls.

"I don't get it," Jessica said, who was also one of the front runners for valedictorian. "As beautiful as her artwork is, she didn't capture the assignment correctly."

"That's where you're wrong, Jessica. Vienna surpassed the assignment. It's not always about taking something literally, it's about thinking outside of the box. You guys all want to answer the questions, but no one is challenging the questions."

It was too early for me to fully interpret all that was around me, but it seemed that Vienna was having a similar reaction. Vienna wasn't having a difficult time understanding because she too stayed up late playing *Gun Man Down*, she was having a hard time understanding because it was her being talked about. Vienna never found her artwork to be impressive, no matter how many compliments chased her, she always ran after denial. That was who Vienna was, and I knew that was who she was going to be for a long time.

Summer after Junior Year

74

It was the day after the fourth of July, and I was getting a phone call from Vienna. It was an odd thing for her to do because we never spoke on the phone before, and it was summer break. I got home late the night before because I spent the holiday with this girl I had a crush on named Jezebel, so I was undergoing my very first hangover. I thought about ignoring the phone call altogether but figured maybe Vienna would want to go bike riding or take some photographs somewhere. The reality was way more complicated than my juvenile assumptions.

"Hello?" my voice cracked as I answered. Puberty pains.

"Hey...Wyatt?"

"What's up, Vienna?"

"Hi," I could tell by the background noises that she wasn't indoors.

"What's going on?" me trying to get to the point so that I could go back to sleep. Vienna awkwardly laughed on the other end. Forcefully laughed.

"Uhm...something really weird happened."

"What?"

"You know my uncle, Gustavo?"

"The one who got barbecue sauce on his vinyl? Yeah."

"Yeah."

"Don't tell me he got barbecue sauce on his vinyl again," I snorted, but Vienna remained silent.

"N-no. That didn't happen," silence increased. "I was coming out of the shower, and I went into my room, then I heard a knock on my door."

"Yeah."

"Yeah. At this point, I had clothes on, but I told Gustavo to come in," she cleared her throat. "Yeah, so he came in."

"Okay."

"Yeah. He sat on my bed and said to me, 'I know I'm your uncle, but the older you get, the more I find myself attracted to you,'" my palm began to sweat so bad, I figured my phone would slip out of it.

"Wait, really?" it didn't. My wet grip forced me to listen.

"Yeah."

"What did you say?"

"Well, he went on and asked if he could show me his body."

I gradually started to check out. It wasn't because I didn't care about what Vienna had to say, but because I didn't want to feel responsible. I knew that I was her best friend, probably the only person who she could place the label on, but I didn't want to be stuck with the burden of consoling her. I've never been in a position like that before that moment. I was only a high school student, and I couldn't imagine what she was going through. We were two very different people. I knew I should've been more present, but my hands couldn't hold the phone up.

"Wyatt?" she sighed into the phone.

"Yeah?"

"Did you hear what I said?"

"Yeah, I did. He showed you his body, right?"

"No... he didn't. I said no, and then he left my room. I feel really weird because I live with him, and I don't know what to do."

"Are you going to tell your Aunt Yami?"

"I guess I have to, right?"

I never found out if she did. For the rest of the summer, Vienna went mute, and I was left dipping in sunscreen during my beach days with Jezebel. I didn't hear back from Vienna after that day, and I wasn't sure if I should text or not. I ignored the problem. I would hold hands with Jezebel, and we would run into the ocean while shoving each other deep into the waves. Each time a wave would crash, it would smack the memory of Vienna into my bones, and I'd rise above trying to float on sunken guilt. The Miami sun never stung so much the way it did that summer, the saltwater seeped into my tongue and decimated my lungs. If I kept swimming, I could stroke back into serenity, but when would I backstroke to Vienna?

Start of Senior Year

I was startled by how long I could maintain my relationship with Jezebel. As school started back up in August, I had a hard time keeping up with Vienna. From what I heard, she was moving to New York City. I knew she was looking at Pratt as an option, but I never confirmed if she got in. I watched Vienna enter and exit the same halls we once walked down together. We even had a locker that we shared since sophomore year that eventually transitioned to a checkpoint. Whenever I saw her sweater hanging in the locker, I knew she showed up to school. There were seldom days where we would collide at the locker, but our conversations were always short-lived.

"What class you got next?" I would ask her.

"I'm TA'ing for Talken, you?"

"Cool. I got Algebra."

"Damn."

"Yeah, only senior in the class," we would both casually laugh, and she would eventually head off.

Mrs. Talken and Vienna had a fascinating relationship. It was evident that Mrs. Talken saw something extraordinary in Vienna. There was such fragility hidden inside of Vienna, so much that it caused her shoulders to hang forward. Vienna didn't have anyone, and Mrs. Talken reassured her that she did. I knew that Vienna felt forgotten, and there weren't a lot of people making an effort to prove to her that she wasn't. Senior year people are so engulfed in their made-up future endeavors, they don't look around to discover the kids who are melting.

A Few Months into Senior Year

"Turn around," Mrs. Talken laughed. It was a rare moment of Vienna and me sitting in the hall together during lunch, we used to do this all the time before senior year.

"Okay," Vienna's eyes bugged out, she had no idea what was going on, and neither did I.

"Here," Mrs. Talken stuffed an envelope in Vienna's bag and shifted her back around to face her. "Don't open it till you get home, pinky promise me?"

I thought about that envelope all night long. I couldn't wait to run into Vienna at our locker to question her about the envelope and what the content was. I wasn't sure what Mrs. Talken gave her, was it money? Can a teacher gift a student money? There was something about that moment between the two of them that radiated a sincerity that I knew I would never experience for the rest of my academic life. The way Mrs. Talken looked at Vienna was the same way a parent looked at their growing child. I couldn't picture anyone else more in need of that than Vienna.

"So, what was it?" I was loitering by our locker, trying to seem as though I was occupied with putting in my textbooks.

"What?" Vienna started to put her hair up into a bun, revealing her beaten up band tee.

"What did Mrs. Talken give to you?" I asked. Vienna blushed, flinging her backpack in front of her crotch. She opened it up, and took the envelope out, handing it to me. On the outside, it read, *Read This Whenever You're Feeling Down.* I unraveled the folded paper, and inside I discovered Vienna's three-page recommendation letter for Pratt.

"Woah, she's not supposed to show you this," I gagged, and Vienna snatched the paper away from me.

"I know," she grinned to herself. "It's nice."

End of Senior Year

Class started thirty minutes ago, but I thought I could at least make an effort to show up for the last fifteen. It was raining that morning, and my umbrellaless hair was creating the ultimate emo swoop. I lunged myself up the stairs to the third floor, and could hear whaling coming from the corner. I saw a girl balled up with her knees hitting her chin, sobbing uncontrollably. I figured she just got a break-up text from her two-week-old boyfriend, but I thought I'd check up on her anyway.

"Hey, are you okay?" I bent down, I noticed her back was shivering, and she was starting to lose her breath. "Breathe, breathe. What's wrong?"

"Mrs. Talken!" The girl cried. "Mrs. Talken died!"

My balance had committed suicide that second. My attempt to console the girl stumbled down a flight of steps. I escaped from the encapsulated case, and wobbled down the hallway. I could see different students sporadically placed throughout the corridor, all weeping and screaming. I could feel my own face start to soften and release tears. Everything in the moment was so blurry, my recollection of it all, and my ability to decipher reality, and what I identified as a foggy purgatory. No one saw this coming because people like Mrs. Talken don't die, they live forever because people want them to. I wanted her to, and I knew Vienna needed her to.

I had to see Vienna.

I made my way to the bottom floor while trying my best not to pass out from hysteria. Dozens of students were hugging their locker, others were linked to a teacher, their heads soaking up the instructor's shoulders. There were so many people out of the classroom, and so many people in the halls, it made me believe I would never be able to find her, but eventually, I did.

I could see her standing right by our locker as though she was looking inside, but even from the distance I was at, I could tell the locker was closed. Her hair hung down her back, her long black t-shirt hung to her knees, and her jeans bunched up at the bottom of her converse. This was Vienna's usual outfit of choice, but something about today made her somber look seem even more onerous.

"Vienna," I called out from the other end of the hall. She didn't budge. "Vienna!"

Her head pivoted in my direction. It was like there was an unexpected delay in her joints, but within seconds she was sprinting toward me. I've never seen Vienna run like that before. I've never seen her face so soaked that even the strands of her hair wanted to wipe away her tears. She collided into my chest and swung her arms around my waist. I wrapped myself around her torso while supporting all the weight she handed to me. Her knees plummeted to the ground, and I knew I wasn't going to let her go. Not like I did before, and if she did fall, I was going to crumple with her. I rested my jaw on her comforting bed of hair, and cried with her. Mrs. Talken's death was hard, but seeing Vienna like this was unbearable.

"I lost her!" everyone else's screeches muffled out in the moment. Vienna's holler swept the building and unlocked my fastened feet. Her eyes lifted up toward me, and I'm pretty sure that her gaze is what finally broke my vertigo. "I lost her, again!"

15
Speaking to Closed Closets
Gerry & Tob

UDoneDidit: Back.
UDoneDidit: Sorry.
UDoneDidit: You there?

GerrydaJew: yes.

UDoneDidit: You want to play tomorrow?

GerrydaJew: I can be so infinite but I choose to be mundane

UDoneDidit: You always see yourself on the other side.

GerrydaJew: sometimes i forget theres another side

UDoneDidit: Same
UDoneDidit: But unlike me you face your disasters. I sit in my hell and become my own devil

GerrydaJew: i like that about you.
GerrydaJew: i like that you can't leave your house
GerrydaJew: one day you're gonna leave and find out that nyc breeds problems. the work to life ratio is not an actual thing here, in nyc you have to work to BE
GerrydaJew: you're so lucky you live with your folks

UDoneDidit: I'm not proud of that

GerrydaJew: i would be
GerrydaJew: i can't even talk to my parents about my depression
GerrydaJew: they think it's an excuse to be lazy

UDoneDidit: When there is evidence that it is much more than that

GerrydaJew: yea
GerrydaJew: im starting to get tired again
GerrydaJew: might take a nap

UDoneDidit: I dont want to leave you
UDoneDidit: Gerry
UDoneDidit: Yo!
UDoneDidit: GERRY
UDoneDidit: Im going to wait here till you message me back
UDoneDidit: Listen man, I know living is not easy.
UDoneDidit: Tbh I don't know
UDoneDidit: Im living my life through a computer screen
UDoneDidit: Im scared of what the world might look like when theres no glass between me and everything else
UDoneDidit: Youre able to be without your parents and I dont think I be that brave
UDoneDidit: I cant
UDoneDidit: Its going to be five years next month
UDoneDidit: My mom keeps trying to have conversations about my goals and plans
UDoneDidit: She thinks I should physically get up and go to CEASE

UDoneDidit: I want to be there with all of you

UDoneDidit: I want to meet you

UDoneDidit: I really do man

UDoneDidit: Youve been my only friend

UDoneDidit: I look forward to talking and playing video games with you everyday.

UDoneDidit: I dont want to lose you

UDoneDidit: Depression is hard but youve kept yourself here for this long

UDoneDidit: You challenge depression

UDoneDidit: My anxiety persistently challenges me when I never signed up for the duel

UDoneDidit: Shit.

GerrydaJew: i've had a casual relationship with anxiety

GerrydaJew: i figured i'd be cool with that until she fucked me

UDoneDidit: Thats what she does

GerrydaJew: if she gives me a chance i can settle her

GerrydaJew: they say that anxiety and depression go hand in hand

UDoneDidit: Does vienna like holding hands?

GerrydaJew: prob as much as she truly likes anyone

UDoneDidit: :/

GerrydaJew: thank you for what you said

GerrydaJew: but it takes time for me to recover

GerrydaJew: and each time gets harder

GerrydaJew: ross is always talking about how we are all in control of what happens in our lives, down to our feelings

GerrydaJew: idk if he understands how much we're at a disadvantage here

UDoneDidit: Sometimes I feel like yall dont go to CEASE for the benefits of group therapy

UDoneDidit: But you all go to gorge down the benefits of Vienna

16
Forensics of the Lost Girl
Chartreuse

I wouldn't tag her as a dancer, I'm a dancer. Vienna knew how to diverge into a split, and hit the ground as if it weren't solid concrete. That was her signature move. All the dudes at the club would shelter their mouths to blind out the drool that emerged. I would chortle at all their attempts, and grab Vienna's arm so she could unsuccessfully wine on me.

Vienna didn't understand beats and rhythms, so her hips would uncontrollably gyrate. Her tiny butt would hit my waist, and my backside was always pressed against some mediocre roughneck, or should I say, wannabe hoodlum. I can't front, I'm a fan of the type. Nevertheless, the guys would always be disappointed when Vienna would lick her lips and decline their one-night stand request. Little did they know, baby was a virgin.

"Shorty with the green hair, what's her name?" some chump stopped me before I could place my drink order.

"Negro, she don't want you."

"Chill, how you know what she want?" he had on a fake Gucci belt, I knew his game.

"I'm her best friend."

"Oh, word? What's your name?"

"Char."

"Oh! For real?"

"For real-real."

White people get so sweaty when they dance. By the time I got back to Vienna on the dance floor, it seemed like I took a detour through the nearest public park sprinkler. I was gone for less than five minutes, and a parade of halfwits were swarming around her. I was only five years older than Vienna, and I always felt the need to smother her with mommy repellent. I knew it wasn't the way Vienna looked that tantalized every underfed creature; she had an unmatchable glimmer. Shit, sometimes it would even make me jealous.

"Char!" this chick was always done before the night could really switch into its pumps and show out.

"Vienna, who you drinkin' from?" I noticed a glass in her hand, pushing a brandy scent up my nose.

"Oh, damn! I didn't even notice!" she fell out laughing, almost knocking herself onto the ground. I don't know why I sneak this girl into the clubs.

I introduced Vienna to my lifestyle while working with her at *Simply Lively Boutique*. Vienna was the stock girl that didn't speak to nobody, and always dressed like she was a 1990's gang-banger. I would come to work every day in my thigh-high heels that made everybody talk, except for Vienna of course. Vienna's little eyes would tug the sole of my shoe until it vanished into a different room. I wouldn't say Vienna was envious of the way that I looked, but I was pretty sure she wasn't used to somebody like me. I don't know what her life was like in Miami, but I knew she was alone here, and that was enough for me to save her.

I didn't think Vienna would turn into the hottest commodity at the club, I thought she was too awkward for that. I got her her very first drink, and once she slurped it down, she was booty shaking on the bouncer. The men at the club yearned for Vienna, and she was hot for them, too, which is why I always kept a good grip on her. It's fun to party, but a young lady knows when to reel it back. I was still good at catching Vienna before she went too far, but there were still those seldom moments, like with Jax, for instance.

"You're beautiful," I caught his skinny white-ass whispering in her ear.

"Back up!" I shouted, shoving his boney elbow.

"Who are you? Her mother?" in that very sentence was where I discovered my dislike for Jax.

"Nope, and you won't be around long enough to meet her!" I knew Vienna's actual mom was dead, but I was talking mess.

"Noooooo!" Vienna slid her arms through the openings of his. "I want him!"

"You don't know him, Vienna! C'mon, let's bounce."

"Just let her dance for a couple of minutes. Okay?" he tried to get me to surrender to his puppy dog eyes, but he didn't know that ain't nothing sadder than a begger.

Something about Jax smelled funny. I was quick to sniff sewage, especially when it's hot, and Vienna made that boy steam. Every Friday and Saturday night, Vienna and I would head to Fat Teddy, and Jax would be there with two drinks in his hand. It wasn't too long before I saw Jax showing up at our job while waiting for Vienna to get off work. Vienna would call me at night and tell me about all the places Jax would take her because he had money like that. Vienna was so enamored with the facade of Jax that she started to stray from actual reality, which unavoidably was herself.

"Do you think he's the right one?" I asked. I was painting my toes with a bomb red color I found for half off. I love a good sale.

"I've already decided that's what I'm going to do," her voice sounded so damn chipper on the other line, I couldn't calculate the current scenario.

"Vienna, baby, listen. Don't just go giving yourself to these everyday fools that are quick to leave once they pluck another flower. You have yet to blossom, don't wilt for nobody."

"I created a playlist," she giggled. There was something about Vienna's laugh that held onto purity, and I knew it was going to shrink soon. "I think it's sweet."

Vienna had no idea that men don't want to listen to anything *sweet*. Vienna was so enamored with Jax's inadequacy, that she made it her mission to differentiate him from the typical dude. Men are made in bulk. Majority of men come out with the same issues and complications as the next man, but sometimes a woman will get lucky and discover a defect. These defects aren't particular to every lady, but the woman that molds well with this guy is supposed to be with him. Jax's flaws don't mix with Vienna's, but she is persistently trying to force them to. I can only warn her of these things, but I can't restrain her curiosity.

"Once you give your virginity to someone, you can't take it back. I know some girls say it's not a big deal bu-" I could hear a tiny sigh on the opposite end.

"It's a big deal for me. Jax knows that, and he understands that."

Our friendship fell off after that. I questioned Vienna about the experience, and she smiled, nodded, and continued breaking down boxes. I barely saw her because she'd always call out of work, and I knew she was ditching to go chill with that freak. I wanted to show up at Jax's house unannounced so bad, and snatch Vienna right out of there. I couldn't play the big sister role anymore, not when she was so obsessed with solidifying herself as an adult. Vienna didn't know that real adults consider the consequences of their actions. Real adults push themselves away from people that dig their nails into the holes we created for ourselves. Vienna has too many holes to fill ,and not the ones that Jax wanted to patch up.

The rain had wrecked my new suede boots, so I already wasn't with the day. Simone was at the front counter looking bored as hell on her phone, and for some reason, that launched the fuse within me. I rolled my eyes and sped to the back of the shop to hang up my jacket. As the door shot open, it held itself on the opposite side.

I walked in, and saw Vienna standing between the small crevice of the wall and the opened door, smirking at me. Vienna's glare told me that everything ended with her and Jax, and my glare told her, thank God. She was presenting herself as a new woman to me, maybe it was the freshly rusted heartbreak, or maybe it was her brand-new haircut.

17
Tyrants Under a Silicone Sun
Ross

All the time I spent at Baruch for my undergrad led me to an unpaid internship at a non-profit. I said to myself, I'd be better off volunteering at a women's shelter, so I did that. I didn't mind it for a few weeks, then it got a little catty. The management office didn't want me there in the first place, they went on about how my personality wasn't the right fit, but I knew it had everything to do with me being a man. I wasn't going to let that bring me down, but the coins I was hoarding in my pockets sure were. The rotting condition of my life was putting off its necessary renovation, and I was too moped to do anything about it. It wasn't until one night I got a call from a girlfriend of mine who just started a new job in Queens.

"So, how much they paying an hour?" was my very first question.

"Sweetheart, we don't count minutes anymore. We talk salaries."

"Girrrrrrrrrrl."

My interview was more like two lost friends reacquainting.

The director loved me the minute I stepped into the room with my secondhand saffiano leather Prada bag that no one could clock. My hair was snatched, my shoes were on point, my pants were freshly ironed, and I was surprised that the crisp didn't cut the seat. Not only did I know I was going to get this job, I thought they were going to offer me a promotion on the spot. Of course, she didn't, we specifically talked about my possible start dates, and what my job entailed. I was hired to be the program co-coordinator for a particular division within the community center. I was looking forward to it, but I knew I was never destined to be a *co-nothing*.

I was enjoying my job. My coworkers were a delicacy, and I even had myself a little office crush. In my specific division, we worked with a lot of broken women, mostly women who recently came out of or were currently in abusive relationships. I knew I was in this sector based on my past work experience, and I resonated with all the women in the program. Often, I found myself leading the workshop and guiding group discussions, while the head coordinator worried about her own business. No, it was never my duty to investigate my coworker's whereabouts, but I wasn't about to be the kid that did all the work in the group project, and never got to pick the toppings on the pizza. I was going to bring it to the director's attention.

"I don't know what you expect me to do, Ross. I can't transfer you to another division now. Halle speaks so highly of the work you're doing beside her too."

"I know-I know. Have you thought about moving Halle to a different division?" I was asking, but my tone was insisting.

"I'm not moving Halle. You just have to work with what

you're given, there is nothing else I can do for you."

What Miss. Thang didn't know was that I could work with anything, and I'm always looking for people that need work. Lou was one of the women in the group who were on the younger side. I wasn't sure how old Lou was, but she couldn't be older than me, and I was twenty-seven. Lou had such a beautiful face, but she had scratches all through and around her body, which made me think about what kind of lesions were inside. She came up to me after a session once, and broke down in tears; stating that she didn't belong in a place like this simply because she wasn't like the other women here. Lou dug her dripping little nose into my fresh button-down, and confessed to me that she was schizophrenic.

So, I wanted to know what I could do for her. My arms could only give a million hugs and never get tired, but an embrace is only a temporary cure for a soul that believes it's alone. When someone's heart manipulates them to ponder about their constructed reality, then that person becomes spoiled. I knew that I could fix Lou, hell yeah, I could. I knew that I could find her a doctor that would prescribe something that would do just fine, but what does that ever fix? All those pills do is reorganize things enough in the brain so that mental functionalities assimilate to people-standards. When people come off those pills, they're lonelier than they were before because it was only a placebo for what they really could've been.

I didn't even ask, I did it. I told Lou to meet me in the tiny room by the custodian closet, and no one had to know. I knew I was taking a risk because I was aware that Lou could feel very uncomfortable with the idea of being isolated with a man, but she knew for sure that my scrawny gay-self only wanted to help. I was thrilled when three o'clock came, and Lou was standing by the entrance pacing beside the door. We sat together and talked. We talked for over an hour but no more than two, and she told me about her life, her childhood, how she got diagnosed, and how she ended up here. I listened to her because that's all I wanted to do. I didn't want to give her any advice, not yet because I needed to figure her out more. I needed to understand her before I can try to evaluate her.

As weeks went on, Lou always met me in that room at the same time on the same days of the week. I started to give her advice on what she can do to not be so stagnant. I gave Lou my number in case she needed someone to call when she felt like she had nobody else, and she appreciated that. Some days it was easier to get a vent out of Lou, and other days, it wasn't. I could see it in the way her face would scrunch up that she would be battling herself in the very moment of our sessions. Whenever her eyes would readjust back to me, I'd grab her hands and thank her for not letting them get in the way. I knew it was hard for her, but for some reason, she wanted to do it for me. I encouraged her to do it for herself.

"I was telling my friend about you," Lou came in on the exuberant side one day.

"Good things, I hope," I chuckled, and she plopped on the seat in front of me.

"Duh! I wanted to know if you'd be cool with her joining."

"Of course."

It started with the three of us just talking. Lou's friend, Jherrica, was battling depression. I did with Jherrica the same thing I did with Lou, I listened. Eventually, we all spoke about different ways to attack depression, what are the early signs of a depression episode, and how to nip them in the bud, as much as a person can. I was able to get some pamphlets printed, and the three of us would read them through. Jherrica seemed to have been improving during her visits, just like Lou. Both of them would come in feeling much better than the last day I saw them, with different kinds of smiles simmering on their faces. I was so sure that I could keep this up without the director knowing, but somehow everything gets back to the boss.

"Do what you want, but I'm not paying you during those hours nor will I fund it. Good luck," those were her precise words.

I knew the program would eventually eat at my time, but I was very thankful I didn't get fired. It went on for several months. The girls invited more of their friends, different people from other programs also heard about it, and joined us for a session or a few. It was an open space for people to come and talk about their mental health freely with other people like them. It showed people that they weren't alone, and there were others in this busy city that feel the exact same way they did. It wasn't just about being vulnerable, but it was about being honest with themselves. I was proud of everyone who was able to admit they had a problem, and were looking to fix it in a communal way.

"Are you guys ready to cease the day?" I would ask before the end of every meeting. The group would shout yes in unison, and we would all go about our ways.

"Cease," Lou said to me. "That's what this is. This is CEASE!"

I was proud of Lou. Lou was the person who inspired me the most to create CEASE. It started off as more of a therapy session, but soon transitioned into something greater. I never told Lou, but I also knew what it was like to battle with internal thoughts in my head, thoughts that never seemed to make any sense but were always fatal to my health. I was always able to walk around with so much confidence that I made sure it sweated through my shoes. Before I got this job, I was battling with my will to strive for what I always expected of myself. With CEASE, I knew I was living passed my exceptions, and I was doing exactly what I needed to do for my health. I couldn't thank Lou enough for that.

I got a call one night from Jherrica, telling me that Lou was doing real bad, and had been admitted into Kings County hospital. I knew what those psychiatric hospitals were like, and I wish Lou had called me before going in. These hospitals will keep a patient if they see an ounce of weakness because they need these patients to run their facilities. The doctors won't do jack to keep them motivated enough to want to even imagine a better future. My mind was heading to the worst places thinking about Lou's mental state, and how she wasn't getting the proper attention that she needed, no one was talking to her, nobody was listening.

When I arrived, they told me to remove all of my belongings and place them into a locker. As I entered the room, I saw Lou knocked out on a seat in the lounging area. I could tell by the way her legs were spilling off the arm of the chair that it wasn't just a tired sleep, it was a drugged slumber.

"What did you give her?" I questioned the nurse who ignored me. I ran up to Lou and cradled her in my arms. Some guy on the opposite side eyed me down, and I aggressively flared my nostrils at him, daring him to do something.

It was about an hour or two before Lou woke up. She didn't seem too startled at the sight of someone holding her, she quickly repositioned herself as though she were an infant. Her eyes gradually opened up to me, and I rubbed her head with my palm. She didn't say a word, I didn't need her to. I wanted Lou to know that I was there for her, and she didn't have to worry about being alone anymore. What I did for Lou was something I would do for any of my babies at CEASE. I wanted them to know that during the times they were going down, there was no need for them to sink. I would be all the floatation devices that they desired, and we could drift off to our own island. I didn't have to say anything, but Lou knew that I'd be there for her a million times just like I'd hug her a million times, and my arms would never stammer.

On my way out, I could see a short girl standing by the nurse's station. The girl's gown fell to her knees, and her arms were crossed in front of her chest. She continuously stomped and screamed at the nurses who stared at her completely perplexed. I couldn't believe what I was witnessing. This young woman was crying to them, shouting, telling them how she wanted to leave and they were unnerved. I knew that if this girl continued that way much longer, they were going to sedate her and she would end up like Lou.

"Hey now, what's wrong?" I was cautious with my movements because I wasn't sure what that girl was in there for or how she was coping.

"I want to go home! I want to go home now!" she yelled. Her face was as red as the bottom of my tired feet.

"You can't go home, especially not when you're acting like that," one of the nurses rolled her eyes at her.

"Listen," I kneeled down to the girl's level. "If you keep hollering and screaming, you're going to be here forever. You have to try to remain calm and relax. Okay? Tell me your name."

The girl wiped her face with her hand and if this weren't the adult ward, I would think she was a child. Her eyes were the most precious shade of brown that I've ever seen, and when her face wasn't stretched out from the sobbing and chanting, she was actually stunning. She placed her hand over her chest to try and capture her breath. I rubbed her back, and soon enough, she found her average breathing pace. I noticed how her saddened face transitioned to a sultry young woman in just seconds. I've never seen anyone that looked like her before, and I don't mean physically, I've never seen anyone who was as hurt as her cover it up instantly the way she did.

"My name is Vienna."

18
The Fishes Spoke Back
Nolan

She gives, and she takes. Always with my own cookies, and I never liked to share anyway. I would rather crawl to the pinnacles of my determination and mimic the way it would crinkle downward. I like to fish for the honey struck drops of carbon that sometimes blocked up my passageways. I knew that if death did this, then death can do anything. I knew that if I was her embodiment of ruptured typhoons and daring stays, I was going to end up homeless a long time ago. I love her though. She is the ideal model for every woman that came after her, and sometimes the men too - when I'm in the mood. My preference is as secured as me, and I rock at my savaged balance.

There we were. She speaks with such a soft voice whenever she wanted something from me, I allowed myself to fall for it too. It was almost like a lullaby when the eyes would soften and straddle good memories. Yeah. This was in conjunction with her lifting a knife to my neck and telling me she would kill me. I tried to stop her before the white dust could touch her nose, but she was so agile. That little ninja was double-jointed and caught particles with her thumbs that I couldn't capture with a net. I always looked up to my mom in that way, whose focus was to reach for calamities and have them ripple down to her own son. No no. Not this time.

We used to play tug of war in her bedroom just to see who could escape first. I don't know what was being strained, mine or her mental elasticity. Who knows? We would continue going for the manufactured gold, and congratulate each other with a whopping of irreversible tears. This was when I learned about music. When my mother won, she would lock me in the room and have me put on her favorite recital, which involved my many blinded sincere apologies. Apologizing for my birth, apologizing for my absent father, apologizing for being disrespectful when telling her I think she needs help. Telling her, we both do.

So frequently, she would get dressed in a low cut top and a faux leather mini skirt to meet her man. I met this man before in the stream of unattainable fixations. He was nothing but a silhouette fully reclined in a car that was too good for him. Nothing weeds out the imposters like replaceable cologne and a broad-brimmed hat. My mother told me she wasn't selling anything, I never assumed otherwise. She boasted about him because he was an opportunity that was needed. That guy was going to be my daddy one day, and just like my dad did, he never felt the need to show his face.

Jesus! We were on the pulpit, arms spread wide, and heads dipped to the banister. We were feeling the Lord. Nothing can get my mom going like a black church. My mom was the prettiest usher of them all, and her favorite thing to do was give people a rightful place to sit. It seemed that everyone was well planted but us, but hey! Who is who at church?

The pastor's grandson smoked weed with me on the back

lawn and taught me how to play the guitar. He was always going on about how many women he was getting, and I knew he didn't have any time outside of church and school to meet a woman. I, on the other hand, was sleeping with several women, some twice my age, and that wasn't anything I was pleased of. I wasn't proud to say that I found a mother in my boxers.

"Nathaniel, what did I tell you about cooking after 9pm?" She was draped in her green satin nightgown.

"I know, but I'm hungry."

"Put the fucking food away!" she grabbed the cast iron and flung it into the sink. The fire on the stove was still burning, and I didn't think about turning it off. I thought to myself, what would happen if I let it burn?

"Mom, what is wrong with you?" I asked her as her eyes pulsated on me.

"Don't disrespect me! Don't you dare disrespect me!" she placed her finger directly in front of the bridge of my nose, and I smacked it out. "You hit me? Oh my God, are you crazy? Please Nathaniel, tell me you're not crazy."

I left her and I re-met her.

I mentioned that it would only get as cold as she allows it to, this woman. I would diverge into the sweat from her back that clapped even louder when my hands hit her smiling dimples. She was a frisky thing. I like frisky, but I don't like when it treats me bad because then it starts to become my mother. I'd pause for a second, remove her pianist fingers from my drawn in chest and bind them above her head. She looked just like a dream catcher when I did that, and I asked her if she would continue to arrest my nightmares because I've got too many already. Rough sex surrenders to me too often, and I am too lenient.

My first song expressed itself as an oppressive ballad that felt sorry for itself. The second was a makeup song for the beginning, and the third captured everything I loved about her. Her name? Can't recall. I loved that she was so open, her limbs regularly dove in contrary directions, and her genitalia spoke to me. How simple-minded was it for me to create a shrine of her body. To recover from her and still overdose on her wicked vibrations, how damned is recovery for a man like me. There's no such thing as a fractured guy with a pure pulsating heart, rib cages don't protect against strange sensations.

"Nathaniel," was all she hushed. I was so far off the ledge that night, I don't recall the process of my fingers creating a stem around her budding flower head. She choked under my grip, and I whimpered as her face turned blue. "Na-than-iel."

"Don't call me that. Don't call me that. Dontcallmethat," I dropped her to her knees, and she cranked down like a de-stuffed scarecrow.

"That's your name! What else should I call you?" She coughed.

"Nolan. Yeah."

I left her. All I had was her car and enough rage to fuel the engine. I promised I'd return to Jersey and give it back to her someday. There was something about New York that seemed so sexy. I always watched it standing there, being full of optimism and potential scrutiny. How typical for a musician to capture his things and drive to a city where the population almost triples his hometown. If I was going to dive off the cliff of my own dreams, I wanted to be the inducer, and I wanted to be the pirate strapped with a sword as a hand. I assumed New York would alleviate me from the women I've known. From the sour woman I've trusted and took everything from.

I met this man with the idea that he could introduce me to something. I was truthful. I laid my expenses out in the most delicate way because when money is sparse, the respect is more considerable. I didn't have anything to my name, I didn't have the eye contact to equal a sustainable friendship. I can't remember the last time I looked at someone and knew I could collapse. This man stood firm with limber arms and a smile so wide that I thought the earth's crust was opening up. I thought that pangea was a real thing, and he was every evolutionary discovery. I met him on the corner of my last salvaged meal. Angels do exist. I guess.

"I want you to join my program, Nolan."

"Why do you want me?"

"Well, let me ask you this. Do you have problems?" he took a bite of his French fry, and I took a bite of his offering burger.

"I think I got a couple of those."

I couldn't live with him, but he was connected to someone who allowed me to stay, even if it was for a little bit. They called me talented. I walked into the place called CEASE with a fresh new shower and a load in my gut. I didn't see anyone else, all I saw was her. I looked at her and decided that I was going to sleep with her, no matter my position. She was the hottest one there and I was going to make it my plan to devour her. I could think about asking her her name, but what good would it do if the shoe was already slipping on before I could find the proper sock. Her short naps fumbled for me, and I could see it in her stare that she was waiting for an arrival like mine. It just so happened to be the right time.

I could see that she was thinning too with very little to start with. We were one before I inserted myself in her, we were like steady flowing antenna signals stargazing about until we sparked something in one another. I can gaze away when she is the focal point and end goal. I knew it! I knew that she too was coming from a sunken disaster maybe even more brutal than mine. She didn't have the battle scars to show, but she had the eyes that ratted her out. I knew she wasn't easy because she was scorched, I knew she was easy because she wanted to be swallowed. I was never a fire-breather, but I can definitely start something. She is not the romantic type, but she creeps for love.

Part Three

Vienna

19
Collecting Hurricanes
Nolan

Vi is so black licorice. She gets jammed in my teeth, and the tartness becomes a staple to my buds. I don't like anything too sweet. She always pondered black souls, and that's why she wants to encapsulate me. Sexy. Her nose shrivels up after we kiss, and I like to see her in a bit of discomfort, which reminds me that she can be something other than robotic. Her feet sparkle and explode each time she migrates; I miss her when she does that. Vi isn't like other things. She spawned from a fissure in the universe, but not in a celestial way. No. She is an abrasion to anything grounded, and cheats the earth of its ability to attract.

Last night, I dissolved in her sweat and kept her perspiration in a locket. She is so beautiful when she is ripped skin and finished with bruises from me. I keep her like a spoon full of reason, seasoned with hypocrisy. Love. It increases with new fossils dug up from somewhere so rough deep inside. I'm smashing more than intimacy, I'm digging myself into wishful thinking. Vi allows me to slip more than just a finger or three into her ripe dialect, and I like to finish her off with all the stress I can't maintain. Where do I disband in her finishing touch? I wake up the following morning gasping for my bad side, and she's off turning it into an art piece.

Her head bobbled forward as she positioned herself up on her knees, falling over her drawing pad. The curtains were drawn, and she preferred to mistake dusk from dawn, and I was always okay with that. My concern held itself in her eyes, the dark wasn't a place to create for a visual artist. I wanted to lure her back underneath the outrageous layers of cotton, and recreate the smells that faintly lingered from our previous assemblage. Damn. The way she slightly bounced on her soles as she stroked the pad made it difficult for me to remain a few feet away.

I couldn't. I resurrected from the sheets and scrolled down next to Vienna. Her chin inserted into her utensil, swaying wherever the pencil strayed. I could hear her subtle but still audible breathing, and it consistently got me off. She was unnecessarily buried in an x-large white t-shirt that wasn't mine, and I knew it wasn't hers either. I reached underneath her bum, and my hand took a swig at the lining of her underwear. She was quick to knock my fingers away, and my jealousy arose. I leaned forward to get a nip of her neck, but as soon as my beard hair scuffed her shoulder, she hunched her back to shield me away.

"Hey, when are you going to come back to me?" I exhaled. She disregarded my comment.

I peeked through her curls to get a whiff of her drawing, and it wasn't much yet, just lines sporadically woven throughout a blank sheet. This creation was unnamable, and I wasn't sure if I wanted to stick around for a definition. Her eyes traced each new line that escaped from her worn-down pencil. I wasn't sure what it was with Vi and art, but she saw something in it that I never could imagine. My music was a fractured universe that I dozed off in, and only my own could keep me in neutrality. Vi once told me that my melodies cultivated inexplicable reactions. I assumed they would moisten her lips, but I never thought they would alter the amount of distance between both of us.

Yesterday, we spoke of unmentioned possibilities. Vienna handed me a squint, and I dashed with it. She wants to doll me up and inhale me as one of her own, her only. She doesn't have to say it, she can just imagine, and I am drawing out her notions better than she could. I wanna know what I win with Vi, besides the labels. She probably barfs coins and defecates confetti. My prize. If I were as romantic as our conversations, I'd submit them all to a ring and make it all mean something delightful. It's easy to get ahead of myself, especially when she's two feet ahead of me.

"Wouldn't it be wild if we were to get married?" I coughed. "Like, imagine me! Married!"

The only feedback I received was a consistent scratch from an under-sharpened pencil. I fell back onto the shallow carpet, and scanned the squiggles that made up Vienna's ceiling. They mocked the lining of my brain, and I could see my glowing rationale transition to a dead battery. It's okay because I know that once the sketch is complete, she will rock to a ninety-degree angle, and apologize for her absence with limitless pecks. I can be patient, I've waited this long to allow love to properly introduce itself to me. My name is Nolan Davis, I am worthy of whatever it may bring, even if she's a little chipped.

Will Cinth despise me for this unbalanced battle? I wouldn't want that because Cinth is lovely. They are also loving, not in an adorned way, but love has meshed with their bloodstream. I see why Vi openly menstruates Cinth and tactfully stuffs me full of cotton. Some of the most wondrous things are kept a secret, and I am the greatest. Cinth comes from bestsellers, and I am lucky if I get acknowledged as honorable mentioned. Don't know. Vi has this weird ability to refuse anything but acquire many things. Sadly, I'm lolly-gagging in the middle.

"Am I asking?" I sprang up. Vi continued on with her drawing, erasing something, and refilling it in.

What about Dell? What is there about her that could compare? On a venn-diagram between the two, Vi overflows with familiar pros. Dell can't understand the fractured and distilled makeup of someone like me. Vi has creaked through similar vacant halls, and Dell thinks that two hands and a whisper could pack emptiness. She wishes that she could associate with the midnight yelps from a mother's burn, she manifests that always. If the sole attraction were physical, I would run to Dell but it's not. I need someone to be defeated with and life has exiled me and Vi.

"Vi! What do you say?" I was puking laughter. "Do you want to marry me?"

Her toes curled up against the rug, and she crept onto her feet, her body was still crunched against her art. Weird. I knew that I could sometimes be a background noise, and as a musician, I know about sounds all too well. I didn't want to fade into disarrayed falsettos, I wanted to be heard. I was being ignored. I tampered with wanting to lounge beside her and pur for her attention or remain in my isolated corner. Vi was the only one dedicated to a spot in the room, and I was attempting to dedicate myself to her.

"Vi," I sulked. The synthetic fiber braised my back and ticked my aggression. The longer I lay here, the more somber I will become. "Vienna Soto."

Notice me because I am ready to rename our encounters and make them equal to something more valuable than the two of us put together. We can turn our illnesses into a swamp of melted validations that we frequently bathe ourselves in. Dope. I want to be the only thing Vienna could cherish and held in delicate hands, I want to be expensive for once.

"Vienna."

She dropped the page to the tip of her knees. Her head flew back, and I could hear the crickets elope from her neck. Her pencil dove between the crack of her ear and temple while the tip pointed directly at me, blaming me. I sat up, waiting for the recognition I murdered myself for, placed my rendered epiphanies on the shag for her. Her head collapsed forward, and she began to daze at the wall, searching for something that was already in the room. I forced myself to belch a few times just to get a glimpse, but she was disinterested. Before my lungs could completely gulp her, she plucked the pencil from her head and slumped back into her work.

She didn't want me. She was telling me without saying a word, and I wanted to know when we became so separated. I can't combine with someone if they are a standalone substance. What was she doing? We were always too much, but we were never enough for one another. No one will adore her like I can. If she wanted to become mute and disintegrate off into her canvas, she could do that all she wants, but she needs to know that I am always on the receiving side. I'm the one who has to live with all of Vi's deported anxieties, she scratches them off and decorates me with them. It isn't fair. She can't fall into her artistry without despair, and I am leaking corruption. Her touch I can live without, but her lips are stained glass that I see my reflection in.

"Vienna!"

I've seen Vi become her attacks. I've seen her sprint off into wherever-land and hope that she'd come out cleansed. She sunk so far into anxiety that an anchor couldn't reach her, she was almost gone. I may have not been the arms that pulled her out, but I was the ear that was present for all the stories. That's how I know we're meant to be together. Shard people like us don't magically fit into this setting. Vi is so exceptional that no one will ever reshape her. When am I going to be given a proper chance to mold her?

"Done," she squeaked. I had almost forgotten what her voice sounded like.

"Vi," I want to finally be the guy she expects. "Did you hear anything I said?"

A cloud passed by the sun right before our eyes met. Her brown stare was always new and delicately intrusive. Her bottom lip pressed in, creating a glistening smile on her face. I collected the brief dream for all it was before I was awoken by a teardrop. My tears never made sense, just like the direction of my thoughts never made sense. I didn't wipe them from my cheek because I was hoping they'd build a lake where I could possibly swim to Vi. I should've understood that she wasn't waiting at the dock, and she'd never be idle for me.

"I'm finished with this drawing."

20
Winding Down Promises
Freddy

This girl came in and looked like the other girl, but they weren't the same. I know because the other girl was a little bit lighter and her butt was more of an apple shape. This girl had nearly no ass but a very pretty face, prettier than the other girl. This girl also had exotic features, she was black, but she didn't have black features. She had…indigenous features; my favorite part was her lips. She has great lips. Her eyes are also a neutral brown, the type of brown that reflects whatever it is they're looking at. I kept checking out my reflection in her eyes when she was down there. I like her more than I like the other girl. I would see this girl again, maybe for her lips or for her mirroring stare.

"Can I shower? I need to shower," I had some blow somewhere, somewhere in the bathroom. I needed to get to the bathroom, to get to that. What's this girl's name?

"Sure," this girl's boobs were out because her dress was half off. This girl is hot, hotter than the other girl. I wanted her to keep going but I needed to shower, I had a gig. I have a gig. It was something for Macy's. I'm doing catalogs now; my agent says it's good.

Should I sniff first and shower, or shower first then sniff? I wanted to see this girl again. I tried to do both, and that didn't work. I put the aluminum on the soap holder in the shower; I'm too tall to bend down so I had to crouch. The shower feels good when it's like this, when it hits me like this. I don't know if it's cold because I usually don't take cold showers. Heat makes me feel like my skin is rupturing, like something wants to get out, to not stay inside. I left the toilet seat up, but this is my apartment. This is her apartment too, sometimes. Not the girl out in the living room with her dress down, the other girl, Caroline. My girl only sometimes.

"I'm done," I came out. She was laid out on the sofa. I bought that sofa. Leather. Good stuff. My friend did it, he does really good stuff. Japanese guy, really smart, makes beautiful luxurious furniture.

"Hi," she was looking at me because she liked me. A lot of people like me. I dropped my towel, and she stared at me. People like me because I model. I work hard on my body. I run every single day. Every day. Every day. Every day.

"Do you want anything? Do you want coffee? I can put some creamer in it, would you like that?" I'm extremely hospitable. "Do you like this song?"

"Yeah, I love r&b," I played it because I knew she would like it, she looks like she would. She would like that stuff, not because she is black but maybe because she is black.

"I love this artist. I love his music, and a lot of people I know don't listen to this stuff," I laugh. "I'm glad you listen to this. I'm glad we have stuff in common."

116

"Me too."

"You're really pretty, do you know that?" I told her, and her face didn't move. It's true, she's pretty. Not as pretty as Caroline. Caroline lives to be pretty. This girl just so happens to be pretty. Pretty met her.

"Thank you," she sat up. "Where are you going?"

"I have an audition for a shoot," I went over to the kitchen area to make her coffee. "My agent got me this gig. He's always trying to get me to do things, but sometimes I think it's better if I go about doing something. Having an agent is tricky, but it helps. I work really hard too, being a model isn't easy."

"I'm sure it's not," she snickered?

"People think because I'm white and attractive that I have it easy. I hustle! I hustle so hard. My parents are both republicans, racist, and homophobic, but what can you do? I can only try to show them another side of life," she laughed-laughed-laughed. I was funny.

"A white man being raised by two conservative republicans and hooking up with women of color is a bit of an oxymoron."

"No, I'm just saying that people only take things at surface value. They don't know about how I struggle too."

"You struggle with your ability to admit that you are common."

"I'm far from common! I have like three hundred dollars to my name, my bank account is empty! People see that I have nice things, like this Louis Vuitton weekender," I point to it under my rack of clothes. It's there. "All of this stuff was given to me. I didn't pay for it, it's all looks."

"Nothing was given to me," she peeps.

"Then, I have to deal with my misogynistic father."

"Misogynist," she repeated.

"Do you know what that's like? To have parents like that?"

"What is it like to have parents?" this was exciting, but she wasn't pretty anymore. She wasn't getting prettier. The more she talked, it became harder and harder for me to be fascinated with her.

"It's not that great, trust me. Do you still want this coffee?" it was hot in my hand, I passed it to her anyway, but she didn't take it, so I put it on the coffee table. Hand-carved from a fallen tree that I found out in Arizona. I drove it back to New York, by myself, all alone. Alone. Alone.

"I think I should go," she got up and snagged her tote bag. Cheap. Black canvas material.

"Why did you come here, anyway? Why would you come here to hook up then leave?"

118

"I was in the mood," she unlocked the door and fled before I could ask her her name.

She reminded me of Caroline. She was just like Caroline in the way that she left. In that way that I don't think she'll ever come back.

21
Chewing Old Gum
Ivory

"Don't worry about the cost, get whatever you want!" Vienna's face hid behind a menu filled with descriptions that I couldn't make out, and prices I knew I couldn't afford.

"This place is a little more upscale than what we used to get," I was mentally deducting the cost of everything from my checking account.

"I'll cover everything," I felt her menu shove mine as she placed it onto the table. "Ivory, it's okay."

I arrived an hour late, I thought it'd be better than not showing up at all. I wasn't going to. There was a sick passenger on the train, and I soon came to realize that that sick passenger was me. I was starting to become delirious in anticipating my encounter with Vienna. I initiated a thoughtless conversation with an older woman who had a shopping cart with her. About ten minutes into our conversation, I realized that the woman didn't speak a word of English. I escaped the train whole, but erupted from the subway grate inebriated with pent up dialogue. I asked a blatant tourist for directions but I knew which way to go, the place that's too good for me.

I've passed this restaurant hundreds of times. Young professionals were always draped alongside the entrance, each of them plastered in name brands that were only available through speak-easy's. I made a decent amount of money, enough to eat at an establishment like this maybe once or twice a month, but I always chose the family-owned business in my neighborhood. The people spaced throughout were all subconsciously mixing their perfumes to come up with the next big thing. I wanted to suggest that sweat glands might be more profitable. I knew that Vienna didn't make an insane amount of money, so her wardrobe wasn't up to par, but for the oddest reasons, she fit right in.

"I think I'm going to get the chicken salad," which wasn't as cheap as it should've been. Also, everything else was illegible through the dim pink lighting.

"Salad sounds good. I think I'm going to get the breaded crab salad," expensive. I allowed my menu to fall, and there she was, looking at me as if I was the one who extended the invitation.

"You look really pretty, Vienna," I shouldn't have said that. I knew that complimenting her was a way of opening the door to a location I wasn't ready to arrive at. As reluctant as I was to compliment her, it was quite true. Vienna always looked beautiful, and tonight she had on a crisp white seersucker dress, and her kinks were growing out beautifully.

It wasn't as awkward as I thought it would be. I assumed that I would no longer have to face awkward positions moving into my mid to late twenties, but that wasn't the case. Adults disregard awkwardness because it's a sophomoric adjective, yet adults are the ones who place themselves in irredeemably awkward scenarios. Vienna was always good as diffusing moments, no matter what kind of moment it was. If I was forcing anything on this meeting, it was tension, but there was none in sight. I thought three years could do that, but time can't distribute itself, not even in a giving matter.

"You look so beautiful, Ivory," I knew she was going to ping-pong the praise.

"Thank you."

"Truthfully, I can't stop looking at you."

"Thanks, Vienna," I cleared my throat, hoping that it wouldn't go any further.

"And you make me smile every time I do," She was good at taking it there; she always was.

Everything was starting to blend, and I couldn't differentiate Vienna from the landscape. I wanted so badly to be in the present moment, to not allow the past to claw its way up. The past always wanted to dictate my senses like it knows who I am now. I was starting to regret every decision I've ever made up until this moment. I shouldn't have answered that text; I should've let my phone ring like I always did when her number popped up. I did it for three years, and I don't know why I decided to give in finally. I was expecting feelings to fail, but they always get by, no matter how trivial they seem.

"Why here, Vienna?" Her hands rose onto the table as she seeped deeper into her chair.

"What do you mean?" she knew what I meant.

"Why did you choose this place for us to meet, after all these years?"

"It's public."

"I can barely see you though," and I was still able to tell she looked amazing.

"Do you really want to see me?" she asked.

"If I didn't want to see you, I wouldn't be here," I leaned into the table while my chest was hitting the sharp rim.

"I don't think I thanked you for coming; you have no idea what it means to me to see you here."

I was scuffling for reassurance. When I told Dom that I would be going to see Vienna, he almost broke up with me. I spent half a work-day in a text, trying to convince him that nothing was going to happen because nothing ever did. He knew that we were moving into a different sector of our lives, and I had to let go of one that was delaying everything else. My talk with Vienna was necessary, I didn't want to do it, but I was given a phone call and what I did with that phone call was my choice. I forced myself to see Vienna so that I could finally see progression in my life.

"It's been hard Ivory, without you," it was starting. I was going to have to come to terms with what happened three years ago at some point this evening.

"Yeah."

"I haven't called anyone my best friend since we were friends."

"It's a hard thing to come by," where was this waiter? I jerked around to see if I could find anyone, but they were all configuring into one another. I couldn't tell anything apart.

"It's even harder to come by someone like you," she moved in. "I'm sorry for what I did that night."

"Maybe we should talk about this after we eat," heavy conversations are never fueled by an empty stomach.

"I shouldn't have done that, but I thought you wanted it too."

"At the time, I believe Dom and I were dating for what? Two years so far?"

"I know."

"Why would you think that I would want you to kiss me, Vienna?" there it went. The starkness of the evening just paid its bill and regret was chiming in.

"I wanted to so bad," she was starting to get emotional. I could barely see her, but I could hear it in her unsettling tone.

"Vienna, we have to get out of here," before I knew it, I was being zapped right back to three years ago.

"I still want to," to that very night.

"Come on," I clutched her hand and walked her out of the restaurant. Her legs trembled by my side and her arms weren't short of the jitters either.

I wasn't sure where I was taking her, but I knew it was somewhere new. It couldn't be a place that I idolized for its exclusivity; it had to be a place where the memories could loiter. I was anxious about the probability of Vienna having a panic attack because three years ago, she didn't know how to control them. They were so spontaneous back then, and I always discovered her triggers before she identified there were any. I knew I had to be gentle, but I couldn't dwindle in old habits, especially not the ceasing night.

There was a small alleyway that led to a very inappropriate playground. I sat Vienna down at one of the small checkerboard benches and placed myself beside her. She was teary, but she wasn't heaving, and that's what was important. I wasn't sure if she was ready to talk, or if words were anywhere on those pretty lips of hers, but I couldn't spend hours hunting for them. I couldn't let Vienna become a priority in my life like she once was, cause I couldn't help but to care for her because I always felt no one else did.

"I can't stay out too late tonight. I'm going to drop you home soon, so if you want to say something, say it now." I huffed. She blinked hard as her eyelashes held onto every drop of water that got tangled up in them, no different to their holder.

"Thank you, Ivory."

"You're welcome," she didn't have to explain. I knew why she was thanking me because she would do it all the time. She used to scare me all the time.

"Can we at least try to be friends again?"

"No," I didn't want to say it, but I also didn't want to leave her with hope. "Our friendship served its purpose in our lives. I'm happy enough to sit here and see that you're much better. You're crying but you're not trying to pull your hair out, or frantically running down a packed street. You've made so much progress since I saw you, I may not be your friend any more, but I'll never stop being proud of you."

She grabbed my arm and wrapped it around her like a wool blanket. Her head dribbled to my shoulder as her eyes collapsed. She looked so beautiful, not because her makeup was more elaborate than usual or her dress hugged her shape, but because she was striding. Vienna was moving forward, and she was doing it without assistance. No matter how weak she thinks she is, she always finds herself shading in the parts of her that aren't well executed. She is an artist, so she's consistently making corrections. Each revision she makes makes her more and more breathtaking.

"Do you remember what I told you after I kissed you that night?" she murmured.

"You told me that if you could feel love, it would be the most tragic thing in the world."

22
Telling on Lights
Gerry & Tob

GerrydaJew: dude
GerrydaJew: yo
GerrydaJew: yoooooooo
GerrydaJew: u there?

UDoneDidit: 1 sec
UDoneDidit: Back.

GerrydaJew: you won't believe what happened today
GerrydaJew: at CEASE

UDoneDidit: Delilah didn't show up.

GerrydaJew: i wish.
GerrydaJew: the day Delilah doesn't show up is the day you do
GerrydaJew: srry that was low

UDoneDidit: Nah I can appreciate the disqualification.

GerrydaJew: Vienna came in
GerrydaJew: And said she's leaving

UDoneDidit: Where is she going?

GerrydaJew: she's leaving CEASE

UDoneDidit: For good?

GerrydaJew: ya

UDoneDidit: What are you going to do?

GerrydaJew: I want to follow her

UDoneDidit: Even you know that's irrational

GerrydaJew: I do but
GerrydaJew: you should have seen her today.
GerrydaJew: she walked in
GerrydaJew: her cheekbones pushing the bottom of her eyelids up
GerrydaJew: and her smile combated each person's mental illness
GerrydaJew: giving us all amnesia
GerrydaJew: making us forgot why we were there

UDoneDidit: To fix ourselves
UDoneDidit: because we all need help

GerrydaJew: i'm not convinced that she no longer needs CEASE

UDoneDidit: I'm sure she still needs help.
UDoneDidit: She probably no longer needs you guys.

GerrydaJew: i'm so jealous

GerrydaJew: because I know that she's going to keep in contact with people like
GerrydaJew: cinth
GerrydaJew: nolan
GerrydaJew: she probably already deleted my number
GerrydaJew: all my chances have been blown

UDoneDidit: Haha.
UDoneDidit: Okay.

GerrydaJew: what?

UDoneDidit: Do you really believe that Vienna wants to be with you?
UDoneDidit: Do you believe shell ever wanna be with you?

GerrydaJew: that's brutal

UDoneDidit: Think about it
UDoneDidit: If she wanted to be with you
UDoneDidit: Shed be with you already

GerrydaJew: ya
GerrydaJew: thanks
GerrydaJew: fully aware of all of that

UDoneDidit: Shed be with anyone.
UDoneDidit: If she really wanted to.
UDoneDidit: But she chooses to be alone.
UDoneDidit: So, don't take it personal.

GerrydaJew: that's just Vienna

UDoneDidit: You have to let her be Vienna.
UDoneDidit: Wherever she goes.

GerrydaJew: i'll never meet anyone like her again

UDoneDidit: That's probably for the better.

GerrydaJew: thanks

UDoneDidit: Np
UDoneDidit: I got something to show you

GerrydaJew: what?

UDoneDidit: Haha
UDoneDidit: **UDoneDidit has shared a photo**

GerrydaJew: holy shit
GerrydaJew: is that you?

UDoneDidit: Yeah lol.

GerrydaJew: DUDE
GerrydaJew: WTF
GerrydaJew: wait who took that photo lol

UDoneDidit: My mom
UDoneDidit: She also picked out the shirt too
UDoneDidit: She got really excited when I asked

GerrydaJew: DUDE

GerrydaJew: damn

GerrydaJew: I don't know what to say

GerrydaJew: thank you

GerrydaJew: thank you for sharing that with me of all people

UDoneDidit: I thought it was long overdue.

GerrydaJew: lol

GerrydaJew: dude

GerrydaJew: you're a really good looking guy

UDoneDidit: You think so?

GerrydaJew: yeah man

GerrydaJew: now I'm glad you never came to CEASE

GerrydaJew: Vienna might've fallen for you

23

Falling into Molds

Esteban

I don't know what she does or why she's always up there. I'll pass through the third-floor hallway just to see if I can hear a shuffling noise coming from the other end. It always sounded like sandpaper whenever she was home, and I assumed it was cause she was rough to get to. I never tried with her because I saw my daughter in her eyes. She was about ten years older than Jenny, but still held innocence like innocence craved her. I could understand why, and that's probably what made her so special.

"Vienna!" I jiggled the doorknob a bit to get her attention. I could hear the abrasions come to a halt. "Hey, I gotta check the pipes. The people downstairs are complaining."

Nothing. Tenants liked to gnaw at my free time and mitigate my mental clarity. It was pretty damn hazardous. Nothing is more perilous than a watered-down super, and I'm tasteless. This one time, a tenant tried to coerce me into sleeping with them to lessen their rent. I told him, young man, I don't swing that way, and secondly, I'm the wrong person to try and get busy with. That's the trouble with supers, our workload stacks up into flights of stairs, and that's why we can never catch our breath. My time would be malleable if tenants like Vienna would quit acting like they're not home when I can blatantly hear them.

"Vienna, I know you're in. C'mon, are you running the washer while you shower again?"

I don't know how she makes a living, but building management never brings her up to me. For her sake, I hope it's something legal, and doesn't involve exposing her character. It doesn't matter how much a bill is worth, it means nothing when it's flung on the ground, or tucked between a cheek and a thong. The time she comes home is never consistent, and I look out for her because looking at clogged drains all day can stump a brain. She's the easiest concern I've got, and that concerns me a lot. The people that don't complain are the ones whose bones lock up from shut-in wails. She looks like she's doing alright, whatever that means.

"Coming," she wasn't even trying to be audible. Some things were moved around, and within five minutes, she was face to face with me. "Yes?"

"Hi Vienna, the neighbors downstairs are complaining of leaks. Do you mind if I come in and have a look?" I asked. Her eyes bobbled around like they didn't know which direction to go, but all they had to do was allow me in.

"Yeah. Yeah, you can come in," the door wandered open, and a gust of paint fumes sprawled through the hallway.

My boots had a hard time leading me in, but they eventually made their way. I haven't been to Vienna's apartment many times, but this visit was incomparable to others. Her sofa, which was usually pushed up against the wall, was smack dab in the middle of the floor. Crumbled newspaper mopped the ground, and her walls were dripping with neon painted lettering. I couldn't make out any of the words because my sight was obstructed by repair costs. I knew Vienna was an artist because I've caught her drawing stuff up in the hallways, but it was always kept to a page. Why did she decide to venture out onto my canvas?

"This is unacceptable. Management is going to kill me, and then kill you in fees. Do you know how serious this is?" I got my phone out, I didn't know who I was calling, but I started dialing.

"You don't like it, Esteban?" I looked over at her for the first time. She was in her bra and panties, cherry colored, bitter. Paint outlining the subtle bumps in her skin where her bones poked out.

"It's not that I don't like it, but there are certain laws that tenants have to abide by."

"I understand."

"You usually keep to a piece of paper, where you normally draw your little characters and scenery, now you got all these words everywhere, none of it makes sense."

"Hm," she waltzed up to one of the words. I couldn't understand anything, nothing was legible, and everything was swollen cursive. "This is my scenery, and I am the focal point of the piece."

"What's that noise?" it sounded like running water, and I was worried I'd run into one of her many guests naked in the shower.

I went over to the door of the bathroom to crack it open a bit. The view I had made me feel as if I was on some kind of hallucinogenics and Vienna was a trip on her own. The faucet was turned up, shooting nothing, but blazing hot water. The bathroom floor was caking up with water, paintbrushes, and colors trying to find their way to some stability. Over fifty brushes lying at the base of the spilling bath. If Vienna wanted to make herself the focal point of something, she was exceeding all my general expectations.

"Well, this is why there's leakage downstairs."

"I had to clean them."

"You're going to get evicted, Vienna! Do you see how serious this is? Look at the damage you're doing to this apartment."

"I need to create art," she stretched her arms out to the ceiling, and I could see her bitty brown nipple poking out of her lace.

"You should put some clothes on too. You shouldn't feel comfortable being naked around strangers."

"I'm the most comfortable being naked around strangers," she strolled into her bedroom, and I could hear a drawer being shoved closed. She walked back into the living room with a plain white t-shirt on. "What do you think of me, Esteban?"

I think she's insane, gone right off the deep end, but she didn't dive off it. She turned her back toward the waves, pushed off, and attached a boulder to her foot to keep her down. I think she needs to get help, not just from a psychiatrist, but from someone like a family member. I think she needs to find someone who will love her properly, the way love should be handed out. She needs to go back to school and educate herself, no, school needs to teach kids how to properly educate themselves. She needs to stop heading wherever she's heading, she needs to invest in a compass or a map. Most of all, she needs to clean up this damn mess.

"I don't think nothing about you, Vienna."

"Really? Nothing at all?" she was tapping her foot lightly like she was dancing a bit.

"I think that maybe you should talk to somebody," she stopped moving.

"I am talking to somebody."

"Someone who can give you advice or something."

"You think I have problems?" I don't think, I know.

"You got some things you gotta get off your chest. It ain't normal for people to go around writing all over their walls," I made my way to the door. It didn't seem like she had any interest in fixing the place up, so I had to be the adult and get my job done.

"Can you stay?" her voice broke. What did I get myself into?

"I'm coming back, I need to get some stuff."

"I need you to stay. Please. Even if it's just for a minute. Please," Vienna turned away from me and started to face her window. Her cat came out of God knows where and braised her feet.

"I'll be right back."

"People leave. They want to be there, but soles say otherwise, they're always wandering. Can you stay? Please. Even if it's just for tonight. Please. We don't have to do anything."

I wish I could describe what I was seeing. Was I witnessing the crack in the brain? The chink that only shows up when the mind can't hold nothing else. Was I witnessing the beginning stages of a creative genius? If this isn't art, then I can't imagine what it could be. Does art bubble like this? I could see the parts of her that can't be smoothed out. As beautiful as she is, she never looked so ruptured. I knew that she wasn't whole. I assumed that she wasn't whole cause she was young, but I could visibly see the pricks in her skin, the places where people touched and sucked, and forgot about. I never witnessed anything like this before, and I hope I never have to ever again.

"We don't have to do anything, Esteban," she picked up her cat, whose nails snagged at her t-shirt. The cat held onto her so tight, the way I should be but can't. "I don't want to do anything anymore."

24

Tweezing Purple Bruises

Yamiles

Vienna,

Is new york treating you good? I haven't heard from you in a long time so I wanted to check in. I went through some of your clothes yesterday to give to some of our family. I forgot how small you were/are. I hope you're eating good. Lora is eating so damn much because of puberty and shit. She's getting a little ass too, finally right? She is doing so good in school too, she's top in her class. I'm sure that she is going to get a good scholarship for college, her teachers tell me that I need to be on that with her. She's getting tall too, like damn, I think she's going to be even taller than you. I'm proud of her and I'm proud of you, it takes a lot of move to a different city and start a life there. You've been doing it all on your own and I wish I could have supported you more with finances but you know I just don't have it.

Lora said you haven't drawn those pictures for her in a little bit. She doesn't like to show them to me because she says they private but she sneaked one. I love it, you're so good at that. Do you have a boyfriend yet? You're growing up into such a beautiful girl, I worry too. I watch the news and there was some guy going around sniffing peoples feet in the Bronx. You don't live in the bronx though but I still don't know how close that is to Manhattan. I hope you're doing good though with your apartment. I don't know how the hell you make a way but you fucking do it. I respect that, you're so much like your mother that way. I miss her. You are just like her, it's crazy. You look like your father though. That dumbass, I can't stand him.

When your mother died she told me to protect you. I hope I'm doing that. She said that you and Lora was her life and I want you to believe that. You were everything to your mother. You especially. I don't think I told you this but before she died, she told me that she was proud of you. She said that you may not have the most expensive shit, you may not be the prettiest girl, which you are turning into, every ugly duck has their time, but she is proud of you. She wasn't always around because she wanted to do her her own thing but she was proud because you always focused on school and taking care of Lora. You never gave up, even when she wasn't around. It's true, I know you're struggling somehow right now babygirl but you don't ask for nothing. I'm sorry.

I'm sorry about what happened. We can't hold grudges with people though because God won't let us in if we do. We have to let things go. What your uncle did, he was drunk and you know that. He was going through some things and him and I weren't in a good place, so he took it out on you. He didn't mean it, he didn't mean what he did and he is sorry. He's a good man Vienna, I want you to call him sometime. You know that Gustavo loves you and Lora and treats y'all like you're his own kids. He wouldn't do anything to hurt you. He loves you, please believe that. Talk to him and forgive him. Time heals wounds, right? Call him, okay?

Anyway, I hope everything is good. I know you don't talk to me too much but you always talk to Lora. The last time you took this long to respond, you weren't doing so good. You have to pray that shit out Vienna, it ain't real. All those demons in your head be talking to you but they not saying anything you can use. That anxiety ain't nothing. Ignore it. I want you to pray to God every night before you go to sleep. Ask him to heal you and to cleanse your thoughts. If you don't feed your conscious with prayers, then it will continue to go raw.

I love you so much, please call.

Yamiles

25
Raising Arms and Altitude

Delilah

It was her last day today, and my presence was insulted by a supermarket cake. The smell that resurrected from the frosting almost gave me a nosebleed, and I thought I would have to quarantine the facility. Ross was too busy gyrating against the belt of his skin-licking pants that he couldn't notice my despair. I dealt with him for about thirty minutes until Gerry arrived looking like his hair was making fun of him. After Gerry, it was Nolan, and he laid an un-moistened peck on my cheek that scratched at my admiration for him. Behind Nolan was Cinth, who always threw a wave at me, bless her. I waited for Vienna to stride in behind Cinth, but all that came through was an irritating blast of hot air. She better come.

"Does anyone have candles?" This was a going away party, not a celebration of life, and if there was any life that needed castigating, it was Vienna's.

"I got a lighter," Nolan reached into his pocket.

"Don't need a lighter, I need candles!"

"I can go get some, but why do we need candles? It's not her birthday," thank you, Cinth.

"It could be nice to have some candles."

"This room has no windows; I'm sure there are fire safety codes against lit candles," I needlessly explained.

The door cranked open, and there she was. Her body sopped up a violent scarlet dress. Her cleavage was so deep; I'm sure glory found its hole in her. Her makeup was bad, and her hair was brushed down to uncover her unadmired features. Her eyebrows were growing like a thirteen-year old's adolescent pubes, and her mascara was cheap. Her breath was heinous, and I could smell it before she opened her infected mouth. I had to cradle my need to regurgitate immediately.

I looked around at the group who was thunderstruck by her easiness, specifically Nolan. Nolan looked at Vienna like he never crunched on her yeast, and I'm still lacing myself with garlic because of her. What they saw in Vienna was something that I wouldn't be able to see with a magnifying glass the size of my head, and even then, I would think I was coming on with dementia. Cinth shows her off because Cinth struggles to show who she is. I'm pretty sure Gerry is a virgin and is thankful to make eye contact with anything female, and Ross wants to be Vienna, which is more than evident. I don't know why I continued to go back to CEASE after months and months of demise, but I can finally start coming for a higher purpose. Praise him.

"You look beautiful, Vienna," Gerry's mouth broke wind.

"Yeah, like, wow!" Cinth.

"Damn!" Nolan shouted then shyly peeked over at me. "Damn."

"I thought it was appropriate," she giggled, but it certainly is not.

My daddy says that if people harbor sour things, they'll stink up everything. Vienna has been the pollution that I've been trying to clear for a while. I've slumped to my knees to pray many evenings, many mornings, and even before I enter the moldy New York City transportation system. I did it all for this day. I never wanted to witness anything more than to watch her overly used backside face the door and exit the room for good. My greatest testimony will be expelling her from each part of me, finally being able to inhale.

"Can I say something to each of you before I go?" please spare us.

"Of course!" Ross dug a smile into his piss colored teeth.

"I'll start with Gerry," I wanted to leave. I'd rather be the Devil's dinner; I'd rather have a steel pipe shoved down my insides and roasted in the flames of hell than to listen to her.

"I'm kind of nervous," Gerry wheezed.

"You are so kind. You always made CEASE a little more lighthearted, which is ironic because you have depression. You never let it get to you, and that's such a skill, please tell Tob I said hello." She grinned, and I held my stomach.

"Thank you," Gerry nodded and wiped a fake tear.

"Nolan, thanks for listening to me, and being there when I needed someone."

"Forsure," he responded. They aren't allowed to talk to each other. What is going on?

"Cinth, you know that we've had a very special relationship and I'm sure that it will continue outside of CEASE."

"It will," Cinth winked.

"Delilah," she began.

It was happening. I felt as though I was being offered up to a herd of falsities. I didn't do anything wrong in my life to be publicly and verbally stoned, but this is how I was going to go. God tests people in the most trying times, and my faith has been on a scantron for far too long. I know that my father has kept me rational enough to not react on immediate instincts. I was being hammered into a wall with a rusted nail, and the strikes weren't leading anywhere. I was being shamed when my stance was never faulty. I needed protection, and I needed to create a quilt of salvation.

"Psalm 140:4, *Keep me safe, Lord, from the hands of the wicked; protect me from the violent, who devise ways to trip my feet.*"

"Delilah?" she uttered.

"Don't." I was almost begging.

"Don't?"

"Don't say anything to me."

"Delilah, that's kind of messed up." Gerry graciously chimed in.

"I'd rather you not, okay?"

I lifted my head at her, and this was the first time we looked directly at one another. Her face wasn't startled because she knew I didn't like her. My reasoning didn't have to match up to a written statement; it was very evident. I didn't need to be poisoned by her farewell to feel relieved; I only needed her to leave. She has tarnished me to a nonreturnable state, I've worked hard to be me, and she disrespects it every time. I didn't have to tell her. She can look at me, and point out any verse that coincides with my displeasure of her. I hate her. I don't only hate her, but I detest everything she thinks she is and wants to be. I don't need her words, and she doesn't need mine.

"Okay," was all she said.

"Dell, don't be like that," Nolan relaxed his hand on my thigh and quickly moved it away when he noticed my dissatisfied stare.

"Don't you dare ridicule me," I barked at him.

"You need to chill out. You're acting like a crazy person. We're all crazy, but we try to change here."

"You don't get to tell me what to do, I'd rather anyone in this God forsaken room tell me what to do besides you!"

"You're freaking out," he whispered.

"Delilah, honey do you want to step outside?" Ross put his hand out toward me, and I wanted to spit right in the middle of it.

"No! I want her to leave! Why is everyone treating me like I'm the problem when it's her, everything leads back to her!"

I pushed up from my seat and stomped toward Vienna. Right in front of her. I needed to study her more, get a grip on why angels idolize her. Her eyes took me in, brown like the root of a plant, the part no one sees, the part no one cares about. Dirty. My strength was the weight that held my hand by my side, I was locking my fingers to my beliefs, and I believed that I was going to mince her. I was going to reveal the sides that only I could see and I was going to do it all right in CEASE, right in front of everyone. I needed to. I needed to, but the weight was too strong. Why was it so strong?

Her hand rose up ,and I flinched awaiting the minute her grimy fingers touched my face. They came in contact, but they didn't hit. They chafed my cheekbone and twitched along the top of my lip. Her other hand joined in as she moved along each protruding bit of my head and up into my hair.

She looped her finger into my hair elastic, and released the batch of blonde onto my shoulders. My strands scattered about, pricked me, and tugged my nerves. I needed to get a brush. I held my breath as her thin hands skimmed along my scalp and ran to the base of my neck. She allowed one of her palms to dive into my shirt and lightly tap on the beginning of my spine. She didn't lose her stare as she did this, and I couldn't stop looking at her even.

I couldn't stop her.

Jesus.

Help me.

26
Along the Vista

Cale

Taresa used to slump on benches like that too. Her body never liked to comply with normal sitting standards; she'd introduce herself to people with her feet. She dangled upside down so much that it became a strategy not to get her pregnant. It became her signature, and I was always able to spot her in a crowd. Beautiful, she was. I never met anyone as remarkable as her, and I thought I never would. Taresa always had an edge about her that made me conscious of leaving her on cliffs. I could always find her bopping off to the side of her glaciers and melting them with her make-believe. I never thought I'd meet anyone like her, and that was until she gave birth to herself.

"It's not good to sit like that; all the blood is gonna rush to your head," I'd tell Taresa the same thing.

"What kind of sandwich did you bring me?" Vienna always got straight to the point, just like her mother always did. We never lasted long.

"Turkey and bread, as plain as it can get."

"The way mayonnaise gets caught in my teeth makes me feel like its lubing it up for things to come out," she reached her hands out for me to pass her the crumbled paper bag.

"Sit up, please," I asked. Vienna batted at me for a while until she decided that she was hungry enough to listen.

"Thank you."

Evening was coming on to us, and the sun was now playing patty cake with the trees. We sat in front of a body of water that crashed at the ankles of the Williamsburg bridge. A slick seagull rode the tide, and his head clicked as each pedestrian stuffed their mouths full of inadequate suppers. The somber saltwater tangoed with my nose hairs and made me forget about New York City. The memories I've held here before moving to Miami were a dismay against the light friction of the waves.

A little girl in a bright blue swimsuit waddled by and stopped directly in front of Vienna. Vienna twinkled her fingers at the child, who bashfully covered her plum-colored cheeks. The parents of the small girl stopped in front of us and encouraged their daughter to talk. Vienna's smile parodied the young girl's, and they were timeless reflections of each other. The parents continued to engage with their daughter and gradually began conversing with Vienna. She usually contorted at conversations with unfamiliar people, or people in general, but she received their presence with sincerity, more so than my own.

"Are you two planning on having kids of your own?" the mother slyly glanced at me and abruptly wheezed. "I'm so sorry! You guys are clearly related."

"That's my father," she's never said that before. She still calls me Cale, and it is rare whenever she does call.

"You have a beautiful daughter," the women's tone was apologetic.

"Hm, she's alright," I chuckled, and the couple continued my laughter.

"It's getting close to dinner time. It was nice speaking to you two," the woman lifted the girl onto her hip, and the group strolled toward the copper sun.

Vienna returned to her disoriented sitting position once she finished her sandwich. A noticeable bruise sunbathed on her skin and established itself as an explicit love kiss. If I were really a father, I would ask her to cover herself up and be aware of where men place their stained lips. I would know because I have a peck that the most expensive detergent can't polish off. If I were to begin a conversation with nags, I would be putting myself in an unbearably deep barrel. I haven't earned the right to tell my daughter who to be because I was only referred to as an accessory in her life. I could place all the blame on Taresa but that would be easy, wouldn't it?

"He touched me," she announced. I was perplexed by the revelation, but I couldn't ignore it.

"They touch," I remarked.

"So crudely," her eyes mingled with the skyline of Alphabet City. It's unfortunate how when a partner dies, the widowed is forever looking at them through their offspring. "I can't help but to paint them in spry colors."

"How else can you paint the ones we are most intimate with?"

"What color would you paint my mother?"

Taresa was fickle. She would only wear earth tones, and Miami was the place that wanted to celebrate everything but. Her smile translated any tinge that was darker than her wardrobe; she was always the most brilliant piece in the room. I'd fall in love with her; the more her colors would shed. What was underneath wasn't just a body for me to feed on; it was someone who silenced the vigorous shades because she was naturally lustrous. I thought I'd never witness another person with the same qualities, but she was sitting right in front of me.

"Brown," I answered.

"Brown?"

"When you mix all the paint colors, you get brown."

Vienna slid forward, holding onto the base of the bench to bring herself up. Her back faced the water, and the sun was nearly diving into the horizon, thereby giving her skin tone a deep golden shade. She looked just like me, but she also looked like snoozed mornings. She resembled agony in its most traumatizing state; she looked like if I blew on her too hard, she'd perish. She was loneliness if I've ever seen it and other folk's desperation. Taresa used to look the same way, but in the same motion as the sun, Vienna will come up the next day shining as if she never drowned herself.

"I made something that I am so proud of," she hoisted her arms out into nightfall and laughed. I saw my daughter really laugh. "Then I almost got evicted!"

"Eviction fits you so well," I laughed with her. She used to raise her arms like that when she was a kid because she wanted me to lift her. I see no difference now.

"It also hinders me."

"Your mom would do the same thing. When she was in the hospital, she ripped out her IV and embellished the room with torn flower petals. She said, 'if anyone is in charge of my death, it's going to be me!'"

"Yes," Vienna allowed her arms to drop, the sun had sunk.

The seat started to become cool. Vienna eventually slumped back, and her eyes drifted downward. I knew she wasn't asleep because she always slept with her mouth slightly parted away. I scanned the fluttering bustle of the city and fled into it. The seagull kept his post on the water, and we made eye contact before he flew off. I felt a sudden nest of follicles nuzzle my arm, and there she was. I peeked down and saw that her eyes were open as she gave me the entire weight of her head. She hadn't done this since she was a little girl, since I knew her as my little girl.

Taresa and I would argue viciously over our daughters. Taresa wanted to be the only parent but had no interest in nurturing. A beautiful woman she was, but a rusted ornament she was as well. They were raised to believe that I was a tragedy, and I believed in that truth. I asserted myself with little pride. I deserted presents, phone calls, and letters. I moved from Miami to LA and started my business without them. I worked to reap my benefits, Taresa wouldn't accept anything. I was by her side every night when she was in the hospital, and selfishly, I awaited her death. I knew that when Taresa would die, it would finally give me the chance to see my girls.

I still hate myself for thinking that way.

It never watered my relationship with them. Vienna and Lora knew me as Cale. Vienna went off to college in New York, and Lora stayed behind with their aunt, who can't stand me because I'm black. Vienna would call me once a year to let me know that she's alive. I would offer her some money, a couple of hundred dollars, and she would always refuse. I was surprised when I received a phone call from her informing me that she was breaking up with her therapy group.

I heard of Vienna's disorder, never from her. Vienna doesn't like to talk about anxiety, and I knew that without forming the questions. I wish I had the binoculars to see into her perforated reality, but I was afraid. If I envisioned the life that Vienna lived, I don't think I'd be able to return to my upright sitting position. I'd live in reversed interpretations because it'd help me decode some of my madness. She, however, revolves around the decapitated minutes in her life and sews them together to make them lively.

The stitches aren't always pristine, but at least they go all the way around.

"I'm tired daddy, but I'm not going to sleep. Not yet."

27
Feelings Full and Ripe
Cinth

The suit didn't fit me as good as it did in the store, and I expected that. I removed the blazer, raised the suspenders, and unbuttoned the top toggle to show a bit of chest. I never thought I'd look beautiful, but I could visualize certainty. Each time the waitress came over, she'd peer past the loosened clasp to read the ink that was on my chest. If I were even a smidgen of smug, I'd tell her what it says. My parents couldn't stop consuming my being, and I'd wipe the sweat from my cheek along with the undesired blush.

"You're officially in your late twenties," my mom poured herself a gulp worth of Prosecco.

"It feels nasty," I smirked. I took the bottle from my mother and filled up my glass, anticipating the dinner.

It wasn't my idea to book a prestigious place. My father sustained a humdrum relationship with the owner and managed to get us a table. Someone with honorable status sat perpendicular to us, and my parents stealthily gawked over every ten seconds. I was turning twenty-six, but I was still on the youthful side of the room, and that's without counting the servers. Our server had a wisp eye, and her lips read me more than my menu options. It made me want to admit my unavailability to her, not to steer her away but to salute myself.

Vienna: Im nervous

Me: Don't be. They're going to love you. :)

The same way I do. Vienna and I were inseparable. I knew where she stood because she was always by my side. Leaving CEASE gave Vienna the ability to think outside of anxiety. I wasn't ready to flee from the group, but it was inspiring to watch the everlasting effects of CEASE. When I'd stare at her laughter, I'd fall in love with the inflation and fall of her gut. She never used to laugh so hard and so rich. It made me greedy for her cackles, I wanted to be them.

"What does Vienna do again?" my father loosened his tie from around his neck, which translated into, he's famished.

"She's an artist," I proudly declared.

"Do you remember my good friend, Alonso Martinez?" There were too many of my father's friends for me to keep tabs on.

"No."

"He's an excellent artist. He's working on opening a gallery in Philly if Vienna is any good, I can connect the two. He is looking for up and coming talents."

"I think he'll be impressed. When she gets here, I will mention it to her."

I over love Vienna. I tell her I love her before she wraps her hair up in a satin scarf at night. I remind her I love her when she's frolicking around the room with her cat in her arms, shaking to no music at all. I list the reasons I love her because I think she forgets, and I'll circle back a half-hour later with ten more reasons. I say it even though she never says it back, but she doesn't need to. I do it for the expression she projects that tells me that she loves herself just as much too.

Me: Where's that smile?

Vienna: doused in lipstick

Me: Can't wait to try it on

CEASE without Vienna is a place of construction. We talk about our issues and ponder outcomes, instead of surveying who Vienna longs for. We were all bolted to her from different angles, we didn't know what to do with ourselves when we were released. It started to become my objective to think of myself without her, as my own person. Vienna is a big part of me, but she is not the fraction that will disintegrate without her support. I see solidity procreating within me, and I see that happening for everyone around me at CEASE.

Vienna: heading out now
Vienna: I should be there soon

She let me contribute to a piece of artwork for her sister. I didn't do much but shade in an eyeball. I was thankful when she asked because it made me feel connected to a page, which made me feel linked to her sister in some way. Vienna was always private, but she opened herself up with small-scaled acts. Her artwork was her inside and outside voice, and I was a microphone that she didn't need, but could easily use when she saw fit.

"I think we should order. Ask Vienna what she wants so we can order it for her," my mother slipped on her marigold reading glasses.

"How is Cinth going to tell her what's on the menu?" my dad asked.

"Cinth has a cellphone, they can take a photo."

"I'm going to wait until she gets here. I don't want her food to get cold." I politely argued.

A small jazz ensemble gathered in the middle of the room. They wore a mix of browns, maroons, and blacks. Within minutes of setting up, they were strumming along together, and blowing into their instruments. I could see my dad look at my mother because this was their type of music. I tapped my feet at the exuberant beat, matching the sharpness emerging from the trumpet. The room was enamored, and some parties sprung from their seats and others wobbled their head. I couldn't wait for Vienna to get here because I was going to vanish with her into the center of it all.

"Shall we?" my father extended his hand to my mother, who coyly took it.

I watched the two of them trot closer to the band. My father was good with his feet, so he led my mother the entire time. My mother wasn't the type that expanded when attention lathered her; she was an introverted writer. My dad was the opposite of her, and that's what made them a wondrous pair. My dad could be the headlining topic of the world, but would still feel unseen if my mother wasn't reading that paper.

Me: I can't wait to see you in that dress we picked out.

It was jade color, and Vienna never looked better in anything else. Even the salesperson was stunned by Vienna's appearance when we were in the shop. The other people in the fitting room handed her compliments in batches, and I could see it in Vienna's face that she didn't know what to do with them. When we got back to her place that night, she took those compliments and made a piece from it. She entitled it her name, but it wasn't a self-portrait, it was her viewpoint of everyone else in the fitting room. Everyone looking at her.

Vienna: it fits well, doesn't it

Our food came about twenty minutes later. My parents joined me at the table, and we consumed the meal together, eating off of each other's plates. Thirty minutes passed by of pure conversation between the three of us. My father bragged to the waitress about my birthday and the profits he made off of my life. I sheepishly explained to the waitress about my parent's success as writers, and this made her want to know me more. I redirected the conversation by inquiring about cake, that was later on delivered to the table with a side tribute to me from the band, and whoever else's birthday it was.

I watched the band chant and shout my way, in the way of celebrating my life. I wished Vienna was there to see it, but after an hour went by, I knew she wasn't coming. I bobbed my head and shook my shoulders while everyone else danced off their meals. My parents were among the crowd of people that galloped around and collided into the groove. I was fortunate because I was there to see it all.

If Vienna were here, we would dance. She'd swing her arms around my neck, and I'd spin her around enough so that her tippy toes would mark up the floor in delight. I wouldn't let go of her until we were forced to return to our seats, and my hand would marinade in her grip. I'd tell her I love her again. My parents would tease our sentiments, and become our personal chorus. I'd look into her eyes and see that she's alright. I'd look at her all night.

"Cinth! I found out who the celebrity is, at the other table!" my mother returned out of breath, smiling and exhausted with joy. "Where is Vienna?"

"She's not coming."

I stood up and took my mother's hand, walking her back over to my dad on the dance-floor. I gave them each a peck on their foreheads before heading out. An elderly woman tried to stop me before I made my exit, and I caressed her shoulder blade, wishing her goodnight. When I pushed the door to the street open, a surge of fresh air swept my face and chilled my clammy flesh. The streetlights welcomed me, and I made out with the city.

Me: I hope you have a good night, Vienna

162

Vienna didn't have to tell me why she chose not to show up. She could easily spoil me with self-deprecating paragraphs, but she decided not to. Her choice was to say nothing at all and treat me with her potential arrival. It wasn't an attack against me or what we had; it was a concentrated motive for her development. She needed this disappearance for herself, and I'm okay with that. Her explanations were always so distinct to her.

And I loved her explanations.

Vienna: Thank you.

Acknowledgements

My sister, Amy Brown.

My godmother, Yolanda Davis.

Chris, for proofreading and co-editing. Also, for giving me the much needed encouragement to continue writing this piece.

Faran Riley, for designing the cover, and becoming a dear friend.

For those who cheered me on, even when oblivious to what they were cheering for.

The Author

Jade Brown has a collection of bunny key chains. She wears a size 6.5 shoe. She has a fluent ear for Spanish. She sleeps on her bellybutton. Don't ask her where the next party is. Her work can be found all over her wall.

Made in the USA
Monee, IL
24 January 2020